# Christmas at Gran Gran's

# Christmas at Gran Gran's

Jana Gillham

Fat Soul Club Media

Dedicated to my parents.
You first taught me how to observe Christmas.

# 1

❧

"'T'was the night before the night before Christmas," Chandler murmured. "OUR first Christmas. At least it was supposed to be." Muscle memory kicked into gear as the highway stretched ahead. *Looks like snow*, he thought. Late afternoon was turning cold and dark quickly. Chandler was a tiny bit glad Sherr would miss this part of winter. It had only been a couple of hours since he held her tight and tried to look brave so she wouldn't worry about him – that last moment before she had to go through airport Security. Bing! A text message popped up.

**Getting ready to board now love you so much!**

"Send Sherralysse a message," he commanded.

"What would you like me to say?" Siri responded in a friendly tone.

"I love you too, comma, miss you so much already babe,

comma let me know when you get to San Juan, exclamation point!"

"Message sent."

"Ah my Sherralysse, Sherr, Shernoble, Sher Khan, Sheribabe." His bride, finally his. The year had opened up with so much to look forward to: graduation, wedding, first job. "And yes God, I am grateful," he sighed. "...but this stinks." It all happened so fast. Just yesterday evening, a little late from work, he opened the door to their apartment fragrant with nutmeg, cloves and cinnamon, a sure sign his wife was on Christmas break. "Mrs. Melotta!" he said in a fake radio announcer voice, "What smells so good?"

Holding a tray of something just pulled from the oven, hair piled up on top of her head, Sherr was preparing a smart aleck reply when her cellphone started playing the theme from *Rocky*. "It's Dad!" she said and threw the tray on the counter, scattering crumbs.

Chandler unzipped his jacket and headed for the tray. Rapid-fire Spanish poured out of Sherr and her tone grew louder and more agitated. Over and over he heard, "*Mamá*," and suddenly lost his appetite for Christmas cookies. Phone pressed to her ear, Sherr sank down onto the faded green couch. When the conversation ended, she looked up at her husband, golden-brown eyes grim with concern. "Mom got a bad report. Really bad."

He lifted his wife from the couch and pulled her close, encircling her in strong arms, but not knowing what to say. Barely an inch shorter than Chandler's slim 6-foot frame, the tall woman sagged into her husband's embrace.

They stayed up late searching for semi-affordable airfare,

stuffed Sherr's bags as if she might be away for weeks and held each other close for as long as possible. Within 24 hours of receiving the call, Chandler was dropping his bride off at the Richmond International Airport.

Now, navigating his well-worn VW beyond the web of access roads, he stayed in "the second lane from the left" so he could take the next exit as directed by the relentlessly cheerful GPS voice. Sherr's mom needed radical surgery to shut down the sudden spread of cancer through her body. Sherr's dad needed help. "That's what you get for marrying a minister's daughter." He mumbled as the VW maintained traction in the growing snowstorm. "Those new tires were so worth it."

The first time Chandler went to visit Sherr's family in Puerto Rico, he realized where her beautiful, generous heart came from. The Palacios ran a center for unwanted children a few kilometers south of San Juan. Orphans, misfits and the troubled found a home at the old family farm. Some were referred by the court, and others deposited by distant relatives. Some just showed up. Chandler wasn't sure how the Palacios kept it all afloat, but no kid was turned away. Some only stayed a few days. Others stayed for years.

Seeing Chandler's dark gold skin and baby dreads, the locals were surprised he spoke little Spanish beyond *hola*, *gracias* and *buenas dias*. Even if he had been fluent, a faint tinge of Georgia drawl would have given him away immediately. Spanish was not prevalent in South Decatur. But, thanks to summers with his grandmother Nonnie down on Orange Beach, he played a respectable enough game of sand volleyball to be accepted by Sherralysse's cousins and friends.

"In one point four miles, take Exit 23 onto Highway 81 North."

"OK. To Gran Gran's we go." His employers smelled money by way of a new development coming to the north-eastern corner of West Virginia. A restaurant property had caught their eye and, holidays or not, someone needed to take a look at it. *Might as well be me,* he thought. *I've worked for those Angelino brothers long enough to know what they don't like.*

Sherr's teaching and coaching salary had supported his final year of school. She never complained, but he wished his part-time paycheck went further. A quick phone call confirmed that the Angelino's first candidate was happy to not work the holiday. If Sherr was going to be gone for Christmas, at least he would have something to show for it.

Dark evergreens dusted in snow crowded close to the highway. Well beyond the city, traffic was sparse and there would be no more exiting for quite a while. Chandler settled in for the drive. He remembered how he first noticed Sherralysse at a church volleyball social. Long dark curls caught back in a ponytail, she moved with ease, giving her team some pre-game pointers. Someone made a comment he couldn't hear, but he saw her laugh and instantly knew he wanted to get to know her better. And he did. When her well-honed instincts directed an expert kill over the net that bloodied his nose and sent them to the emergency room.

"I forgot it was church volleyball. I always play to win," Sherr groaned.

"...and we've been together ever since," they would often say in unison when telling their story.

Chandler liked to add, "I won that game," which made

everyone around them either smile or fake vomit. *Yes, Sherralysse. Volleyball brought you here, but your dad has called you to come home. I hope your mama gets better really soon, so you can come home to me. God, am I selfish? But I think you understand.* Older memories surfaced as Chandler began to think of life before Sherr. So much had changed. *And yes, Grandma Nonnie, you were right. And you never gave up on me.*

"Take the exit!"

"OK, OK, I got it." He swerved the VW to the right and followed the prompts guiding him around a bend, up a hill and into the parking lot of a long low wooden building. Winter daylight was long gone. His headlights illuminated a wide porch and boarded up windows. *Let's see if any of these work.* He pulled a set of three keys from the side pocket of his backpack. *OK Angelino Brothers. So far I can tell you, it's dark.* Chandler unfolded his lanky frame, happy to stretch. *And cold. Should have worn that heavier jacket—Sherr was right.*

He left the headlights running. A sign hung cock-eyed above the door. "Gran Gran's. Well, there is some brilliant branding," he said. The second key worked after wrestling it a bit and wishing for WD40. The bruised wooden door creaked open. "No lights, I'm sure ..." He reached for the switch. It worked.

## Chapter 2

*onder who's been paying that light bill. Angelino's must have turned it on. Guess they're serious. This place is serious—what a mess.* Tables of all shapes and sizes were scattered in no particular order. He looked to the right and saw a mish-mash of ladder-backed chairs stacked against the wall. On the other side squatted a vintage pump organ—decorated in scroll-work and dusty cherubs. All sorts of antique implements and musical instruments decorated the walls and hung from the ceiling. "I guess they were really going for rustic," he mumbled.

Chandler was drawn to the organ. It reminded him of his grandmother. *She would know just what to do with all of this.* He brushed the cobwebs from the stops above the keyboard. Reed. Flute. Trumpet. Bending down he gave the pedals a pump, which stirred up a whole cloud of dust. "OK—need to get this done. That snow is not quitting anytime soon." Chandler pulled out his cellphone and began dictating. "Let's go top to bottom. Ceiling. Hard to see. There is so much stuff hanging from it—how could you tell if it leaks? Lots of spots on the floor—but—this was a restaurant. We're gonna have to get somebody up on the roof to check for sure." *They'll love paying for that—ha.* "OK, walls. Tuba, guitar, accordion, snow-shoes, oilcan, fishing rods. A canoe? Antique photographs.

Somebody's ancestors." He scanned from ceiling to baseboard, zooming in and capturing pictures with his phone.

"Not many electrical outlets, and those are pretty old. Wooden floors. Pine? Lots of stains and scratches, must have been a pretty busy place." *They won't care about any of that. Just the facts.* "What about furniture?" He reviewed the sitting area, nodding his head as he counted. "Sixteen tables. Sixty-one chairs. Grates. I guess there's a basement or crawl space too. Oh yeah—and one pump organ. All dusty."

Scarred red double doors swung open into a medium-sized kitchen. Chandler knew what it was like to push through doors like this loaded up with steaming trays, or later, stacks of dirty dishes. He flicked a switch and fluorescent lights buzzed and blinked on. Fridge. Grill. Great big frying station, warming ovens. *Mmm biscuits, gravy... I need to stop now.* It was easy to imagine this kitchen full of flying hands and feet and lots and lots of banter. *Oh yes.* He lifted up a blackened fry basket. *And grease.* A narrow shelf set too high for anything else held some old softball trophies, a couple of framed photos and a rag doll.

He opened a door marked "Emergency Exit." It led to dumpsters and whatever else might be out back. It was hard to see. Maybe some kind of shed. Chicken coops? It was cold enough without letting snowy air blow in. *Good enough.* As Chandler slammed the door shut, he heard a muffled, scratchy voice.

"Hello?" came from the dining room.

*Gran Gran? Are you still here?* The voice sounded old. Chandler's skin immediately pricked up into goose bumps. He switched off the light.

"Is anybody here?" the voice repeated.

"Bad idea," scratched another voice.

"No, no, there is a car parked outside and the kitchen light was on just now. Someone is here. I know they are."

*Gran Gran and friends?* They sounded harmless, but ... *C'mon Chandler, pull yourself together. Whoever they are, they're trespassing and you are in charge. What'll the Angelinos think if you can't manage a trespasser? Besides—they sound pretty old.*

"Hello? Hello? Can you please help us?" the voice wavered. Squaring up his shoulders, Chandler plunged through the double doors back into the dining room.

Two ancient women, stooped and clinging to one another, fell back against a table. Almost gaunt and pale, they looked very much alike, but the one in the red coat seemed less frail.

"Oh dear, have you got a gun? Please don't hurt us young man, we saw the light from the highway and came in from the storm. We have money ..." The woman in the red coat began digging around toward the bottom of her handbag.

"Are you two alone?"

"Yes."

Chandler sighed and said, "Me too, and there's no gun. Please have a seat."

When the two women remained frozen in fear, his expert instincts kicked in. He hooked two chairs from the stack and ran his sleeve across a tabletop. "Please Ladies, do have a seat. My name is Chandler." He almost finished with, "and I'll be your server," but caught himself just in time.

"Oh, thank you, thank you." One looked at the other and said, "Mighty dusty." Chandler pretended not to hear. The women sat. He grabbed another chair for himself.

Chandler leaned across the table. "So, my dear ladies, this place is not open—but how can I help?"

"What do you mean it's not open?" the woman in red seemed to be the spokesperson.

"Well, it's been closed for years—but my employers sent me up from Richmond to take a look at it."

"So it *is* open."

"Oh no ma'am, it is not."

"The sign is on."

"Oh no, it's not."

"But it *is*. We saw it from the highway, that's why we came up here to get out of the weather—we couldn't see to drive anymore." Chandler shuddered at the thought of these two behind a steering wheel.

"Well, I didn't turn the sign on," he said.

"We saw it and came right up. You've got to let us stay— this weather is terrible."

"I just got here myself a little while ago. I don't even know if the water works."

"'Any shelter in a storm' they say." The lady in the red coat smiled for the first time. Chandler thought of his grandmother and knew he didn't stand a chance.

"Well, you can stay until there's a break in the weather. We aren't too far from Hagerstown, I'm sure there are hotels there."

"My name is Elsa." The woman extended a gnarled arthritic hand across the table. Chandler took it with care and gave it a gentle shake. "And this is my sister Etna. She doesn't talk much."

Etna looked at Chandler through blurred gray eyes and said, "It's dusty."

"Nice to meet you too," he replied.

An official voice interrupted them. "The National Weather Service ..." Chandler set his phone on the table so they could all hear it. The two ladies leaned over to listen. "... has issued a severe storm warning for West Virginia, Southern Pennsylvania, Maryland and eastern Ohio. Roads will become slick, hazardous and impassable. Motorists are advised to find shelter immediately until roads can be cleared."

"That settles it," Elsa chirped. "Young man, would you mind helping us with our things? Looks like we're bedding down here." Before Chandler could protest, she handed him the fob for a Tesla. "The overnight bags are in the back seat. That should be all we need—oh, yes, and there are a couple of extra blankets in the trunk. Bring those too please, dear."

"Yes ma'am."

As Chandler opened the front door, he heard Elsa say, "No worries Ettie, we'll be fine, that young man is heaven sent. I can tell."

The front door pushed open into a night filled with white. Chandler could barely discern the outline of a car parked near his VW. Fluffy white snow swirled around him. He realized he would need to figure out a way to heat the building. A new list of tasks brought on by the arrival of unexpected guests crowded his mind, but first—the Tesla. Oh that new car smell. The sleek black leather interior was almost visible beneath the clutter of old lady travel. An atlas, travel pillow, empty water bottles and a thermos filled the passenger side. Two tattered golden crocodile valises of bygone elegance took up the small back seat.

"That's what we need." He grabbed the front seat items as well and wrestled it all up the steps and across the porch. Then he went back for the blankets. One press of the fob opened the trunk to reveal two blankets, pillows, books and a lamp neatly tucked away in a cardboard box on the left side. The right side was jumbled up with underwear, socks, costume jewelry and a large assortment of medications, as if someone had emptied the contents of a dresser drawer.

Chandler tried not to think about packing Sherr's luggage into the VW just a few hours ago. How long would she need to stay with her family? *I should have gone with you. What was I thinking?*

Chandler grabbed the box and slammed the trunk shut— just in time to hear the roar of a motorcycle.

# Chapter 3

"Hey!  This place open?"  A massive figure dressed all in black climbed off a massive Harley.

"Uh... not really."

"Well, the sign was on."

Chandler didn't wait for the man. Miss Elsa and Miss Etna needed their things and he was cold. The big guy could fend for himself. He let himself back in the front door.

"Miss Elsa?"

The room was empty. "Must be checking out the restroom or something." He placed the box on the table. The motorcycle rider stomped in, kicking snow off his heavy boots.

"Sorry, this place isn't open."

"Whaddaya mean?  The sign is on. And that snow ain't gonna stop anytime soon."

"I know. I know, but if my bosses find out ..."

"This isn't your place?"

"No. They sent me up here to take a look at it."

"Hey—I have to get out of that," the man said, pointing behind him.

"I don't even know if the water's on. I just got here a bit ago."

"Traveling with your grandma?" The motorcyclist pointed to a package of Depends, "Or are those yours?"

"Young man?" A wavery voice called from the hallway, "Young man, would you come here please?"

"Look, these two old ladies saw the sign too. I need to see if they're OK. Just don't touch their stuff."

The motorcyclist smirked. "Yeah, like I need any of this."

Chandler left him and hurried down the hallway. He found Elsa riffling through a storage cabinet.

"Look here!" She beamed. "The gods be praised. Toilet paper!" And sure enough, a few rolls sat far back on a dusty shelf.

"It's pink?" said Chandler.

"Oh yes, that used to be all the rage, but nowadays they've lost all sense of color. You can only find white. In my day ..."

"Uh ma'am, someone else has arrived. I need to go check on him. Have you noticed if there is water?"

"Well, it's certainly not hot, but yes. Excuse me, I need to go see how Ettie is doing." The woman returned down the hall, clutching two pink rolls of toilet paper.

Relieved, Chandler nodded and returned to the dining room. The motorcyclist was now standing in a puddle shaking out his soaked parka. He was not quite as tall as Chandler but very sturdy. Stout. In his shaggy black hair, beard and leathers, Chandler thought he looked like a pirate—one to handle with care.

"It's cold in here man. We need to get some heat going."

"Yeah—no telling what kind of system they've got," Chandler replied.

"Well at least there's a fireplace ... and a bunch of old chairs we can hack up if we have to." The man glanced around the room.

Chandler could see himself explaining to the Angelinos. "And there was this big pirate guy on a Harley who said ..." No. Better to see if he could figure out the furnace. "Hey what's your name?"

"Mike."

"Nice to meet you, Mike. You know anything about old furnaces?"

"Ha! That's your problem man—or your boss's."

Chandler folded his arms across his chest. "Well, I don't care what the sign says. We're not open, I have two little old ladies to take care of and we're not chopping up furniture—yet."

"OK, OK—I getcha. And since we're introducing—who are you?"

"Chandler. Melotta."

"OK Chan Man—you got it. Let's find this thing."

Shuffling footsteps returned from the restroom hallway. "That water in the bathroom is very, *very* cold, young man."

"Yes Ma'am—we'll see what we can do about it." Chandler gave Mike a glance. He was peering at the walls, looking behind framed photos and an old calendar. He shoved a chair aside.

"Hey—look, here's a grate." Mike called out. "My mom has grates like these in her house in Pittsburgh. There's probably an entrance to the crawl space or basement out back."

"That's where they deliver the coal," said Elsa. "Back in the day ..."

Chandler interrupted. "Why don't you ladies wrap up in the blankets and try to get comfortable? It may take us a while to make this thing work."

"Us?" growled Mike.

"Us. I need your help."

"There's a back entrance through there," he pointed at the double doors. Mike headed for the kitchen while Chandler settled the sisters as best he could. He nodded and smiled as Elsa continued to rattle on about coal deliveries, the bin and the shovel while Etna occasionally chimed in, "Dust."

*Yes, lots of dust—we ARE dust.  OK Blackbeard, don't get too far ahead of me.*

*****

Mike was already out the back door. He was pushing through the brushy branches of a small tree that blocked a low door beside the entrance. Drifting snow had already piled up so high you could only see the top edge of the door. "I almost didn't see this. Good thing I had my flashlight."

Chandler helped him clear away the branches and snow. They finally found a heavy-duty latch. It was fastened with a forbidding rusty padlock.

"You gotta key for that?" asked Mike.

Chandler pulled the set of keys out of his pocket. He chose the oldest looking one on the ring, "Let's see..." it did not fit. He tried another, "These all look too new."

"Maybe it's in the kitchen somewhere?" Happy to be out of the blowing snow, the two returned to the kitchen and started opening drawers and cupboards.

"What's all that noise?" Elsa's scratchy voice carried in from the dining room.

"No worries ma'am—we're just looking for the key to the basement."

"Did you look beside the door? There's always a hook beside the door," she called out.

Mike got there first. "I found it!"

"Excellent work boys."

Chandler rolled his eyes and steeled himself to go back out. The temperature was dropping and the icy air made his nostrils tingle. Mike took the lock in his gloved hand and shoved in the key. It turned. "Whew—I thought we were going to have to saw that hasp off." The heavy wooden door was stuck. They managed to loosen it, then nearly fell headlong down cement stairs when it popped free at the last minute.

"Where's that flashlight?" Chandler panted.

Mike pulled the tiny instrument from his chest pocket. It revealed a flight of steps going down. "Go on," he said.

"You've got the light."

"I'll hold it right here behind you."

"Sure. Thanks." Chandler moved slowly down the narrow stairs, trying to ready himself for whatever might have taken up residence. "Ouch!"

"You OK?" asked Mike.

"Hit my head on a beam."

"OK man be careful. I don't wanna have to drag you outta here." Rubbing his head, Chandler moved into the basement area. He estimated the ceiling was not quite seven feet. Mike bumped into him.

"Hey—watch out."

"There it is." Mike shined his flashlight onto a big, black, squatty stove. Fat round arms, which were really air ducts, branched up and around to grates above. Cobwebs, caught here and there by the stab of light, wavered in the musty air. "That, man, is an octopus—the real deal," said Mike.

"I guess it's the original,"

"My mom had one. It's a beast."

"Coal-fired?"

"Oh yeah." Mike pointed the light at a dirty, rusty shovel leaned up against the crumbly masonry wall.

"See any coal?"

Mike shot the flashlight beam around the space. It was not much bigger than a large walk-in closet. "Nope."

Chandler kicked the octopus. His boot thumped on metal. "Well, this thing is useless then." The Angelinos would not take kindly to antique chairs chopped up for kindling especially by uninvited and nonpaying customers. *There goes my bonus.* Chandler took off his gloves and ran his hands over the cold, dusty stove. Then he leaned down over its belly feeling his way. "Where is the door on this thing?" His hand struck something. "Hey, give me some light. See that?"

Mike joined him and both said at once, "Gas!" A small single burner pointed up into the dusty guts of the old coal stove. Someone along the way had converted from coal to natural gas.

"Where's the meter? I bet we can turn this thing on!" Mike rushed back up the stairs with Chandler close behind. Once upside, they frantically began shoving their way through the snow piled up against the side of the building. After a few cold minutes, Chandler located the gas meter a few feet beyond the other side of the basement door. There was the magic valve that would connect them to heat. And there hung another padlock.

Shiny, new and formidable. Mike looked at Chandler. They nodded at each other.

"You know we could get a ticket for this," Mike said.

"Yep."

"There's an old saw hanging on the wall in there." The big man hesitated.

"Let's give it a try," said Chandler. *Let's hope the judge agrees that old ladies dying of cold trumps a misdemeanor.* The two banged back through the kitchen double doors. Mike unhooked a rusty saw that hung below the picture of a chicken.

"Do we have heat yet?" Elsa asked. She tucked the blanket tighter around her sister with one hand while clutching her coat close with the other.

Chandler glanced at Mike who was heading back through to the kitchen "Well, not quite yet. Looks like they converted the furnace to gas. If we can get that turned back on, there's a chance." Elsa nodded. Her sister Etna sat drooped to one side, eyes closed, spittle collecting in one corner of her mouth.

"I, uh, need to get back out there to help."

"It's quite all right, young man, we knew this was going to be a hard trip." She reached over to pat Etna's mouth dry and was met by a brief sputter.

Back out in the snow-filled darkness, Chandler found Mike sawing away at the hasp. "Won't go. Won't go," he muttered over the rasp of metal scraping metal.

"Here let me try."

Mike handed him the saw. The blade was too big and the space was too small. Chandler's arm began to burn, but he kept on even though his effort seemed useless. Mike took the saw back and put his weight into it. They continued to trade back and forth for what seemed a very long time in the cold, but still all they could see was the beginnings of a tiny scratch. "They don't want people to tap into this stuff for free, that's for sure," said Mike. "I don't know if we're gonna get through it."

For the first time in the whole evening, Chandler felt afraid. It was one thing to show up, do a quick scan and drive away—but now there were other people involved. Lives on the line. Should he pack the sisters into his car? Could Mike follow on his motorcycle? Visibility was only getting worse. Would anyone find them? Images of four stiff bodies slumped in chairs was not comforting. *God? Was this your plan? We need some help!*

Panting, Mike said, "It's no use. I could do this all night and that hasp would not come off. I think we're gonna have to burn chairs man."

Chandler nodded. "OK. Let's see what we can do." Heads hung low, they sloshed back through the snow, into the kitchen, past the puddles and mess and back through the double doors into the main room. Elsa and Etna were no longer alone.

## Chapter 4

Two bundled up figures in puffy yellow anoraks stood by the sister's table. Stray gray wisps peeked from beneath matching yellow stocking caps.

"Who are you?" demanded Mike.

"Excuse me?" one of them said. It was a woman's voice. Her companion doubled up fists and stepped toward Mike. They were both much shorter, but plenty sturdy.

"Now, now," said Elsa. "We have just been getting acquainted. Everyone settle down. These are fellow travelers come in from the snow. They saw the sign."

"We need to turn that sign off," Mike said.

"Miss Sydney and Mr. Stanley. Is that right?" Elsa beamed. "And this is ... is ..." she gestured, waiting for an answer.

"Mike."

"And our host, this dear young man ..."

"Chandler, Chandler Melotta." Chandler extended his hand in greeting. The female figure shook it, the other, arms crossed, remained focused on Mike.

"Yes, Chandler," smiled Elsa. "Like a candlemaker, how lovely."

"You folks are welcome to take shelter, and the water is on for the moment, but it's really cold, so I don't know for how long, and there is no heat."

"We should go on up the road," said the man in a voice that resembled the woman's, just a tone or two lower.

"No Stanley, we are not. I already told you. That air is thicker than pea soup. As Dad would say ..."

"Yeah, yeah, I know. Your dad. Weather master." Stanley rolled his eyes, then looked around. "We'll take that corner over there." He pointed to the area beside the pump organ. "Let's get our stuff. I could use some help." He looked at Sydney. She looked away. Mike suddenly became busy peering behind a picture frame on the wall. "Miata? Is that your name? Give me a hand?"

Chandler pulled his coat close. "C'mon, let's go. It's not getting any warmer out there." He tried not to give Mike a dirty look, but one may have slipped out.The snow had blown up so high the VW was half buried. The Tesla was not far behind. Chandler followed Stanley to a sleek, black vehicle. "I'm not much of a car guy," he said, "but is that a Bentley?"

Stanley nodded, "Yep. Picked it up a couple of years ago. Liked my old one better. Wish I hadn't traded it in."

"Uh, sure. I understand."

"Here—let's grab these. Glad we updated our emergency kit. Must always be prepared." Stanley handed Chandler a couple of blankets neatly rolled and secured with bungie cords, then loaded him up with two backpacks from the back seat. From the trunk, which was otherwise empty, he  extracted a large battleship-gray, hard-sided plastic case. "Rations," he said, thumping it like a ripe watermelon. "You never know." They lugged the gear up the steps, across the porch and in, banging the door as they went. Stanley pointed at the corner beside the pump organ. "Over there." Chandler obeyed. He felt the tickle of his phone buzzing in his right pocket.

"Please be Sherr," he prayed as he wrestled the phone out, biting a glove off one hand in the process.

**Here! Tried to call. U ok?**

He yanked the other glove off and blew on his fingers before finger-thumbing a reply. **Crazy night. Will tell u all about it. Lots of snow and guests.** He ended it with the prayer hands emoticon—times three. *The way this is going, she'll probably get that in February.* He rejoined the group. "That was my wife. She just arrived in Puerto Rico."

"Ah San Juan. Remember Ettie? Papa was going to take us. Remember all those brochures? And *West Side Story* had just come out?"

Etna did not respond. Elsa tried again. "Ettie, remember the beautiful picture of the beach with turquoise water and the palm trees?" She returned her gaze to Chandler. "She's just not there sometimes." Then she brightened, "But do tell me about your wife, she must be lovely."

Mike groaned, "Look, Miss Elsie, I am sorry, but we don't have time for stories. We've got to figure out a way to warm this old place up."

Elsa folded her hands in her lap. "You're right young man, stories later. Please forgive a romantic old woman."

Stanley and Sydney returned to the table. Chandler suppressed a grin. They reminded him of matching middle-aged Weebles, set free from the "Ski Village" set.

"Pull up some chairs everybody. We need to take stock of this situation," Sydney said as she pulled a pair of dime store reading glasses out of her vest pocket. She adjusted them below the gray fringe of wiry bangs that protruded from below her cap. Opening a coffee-stained notebook, she wrote the date and time at the top of a page. Her tone was matter of fact. They could have been in a high-tech conference room planning a software release, space shuttle launch or the annual holiday bash. Chandler dragged another table across the scratched floor to join the sisters while Mike and Stanley pulled more chairs over.

Tapping her pen on the page, Sydney looked around at the group and said, "Let's start with what we know. First, there's a really bad storm." Mike rolled his eyes. "It could go on for days. But, we have electricity."

"We have water," said Elsa.

"Cold water," added Chandler "and cellphone service at least for now."

"We'll talk about what we don't have in a minute. Let's stay focused on what we do have."

"Dust." Etna surprised them all and Elsa rewarded her with a pat on the shoulder.

"Yes." Said Sydney rolling right along, "Plenty of dust and ..."

Mike stood up, nearly knocking over his rickety chair. "Look, I don't see the point of all this. We've gotta whole kitchen full of stuff in there." He gestured at the walls, "And there's a tuba and an accordion. Woohoo. How's all that stuff gonna help us get outta here, little lady?"

Stanley bristled and doubled up his fists below the table. Sydney paid no attention to either man as she continued making her list.

"We have rations," she said.

"WE have rations," said Stanley.

"We have brandy," said Elsa.

"I have a coupon for a Seven Eleven Big Gulp," Mike mimicked Sydney's tone.

Stanley stood up, glaring at the man who was nearly twice his height. Sydney ignored them both and turned the page in her notebook. She tapped her pen on the paper and looked around the group.

"Now let's talk about what we *don't* have."

"Heat." Mike, Elsa and Chandler answered in unison. Sydney wrote "heat" in block letters and underlined it.

"There's an octopus furnace me and Mike were working on just now," said Chandler. "Someone converted it to gas—but we can't knock the lock off the meter."

"What did you do?" said Stanley.

Mike slumped back into his chair with a scowl.

Chandler answered, "We tried to hack it off. It's pretty new. But all we had was this old saw. It's no good. Mike here worked on it quite a while."

Stanley stood up. "Let me take a look."

"Knock yourself out man," said Mike. "I'm not going back out in that cold."

Chandler replied, "Let me borrow your flashlight." Mike tossed it over the table and Chandler caught it. Pulling his coat close, he and Stanley went out to look at the gas meter.

# Chapter 5

A very few moments later the two men returned, stomping off the snow, stripping off gloves and rubbing their hands for warmth.

"Who's got some sandpaper or a file?" asked Stanley.

"Like I travel with my woodworking kit," Mike muttered. Sydney continued to scrawl notes.

"Maybe there's some steel wool in the kitchen," said Chandler and went to look. They soon heard cupboard doors bang and drawers slam.

"What do you need it for?" asked Elsa.

Stanley's voice softened. "Well Ma'am, the gas company put that specific lock on to protect from thievery. You can't just saw it off. It's coated with chromium. Based on its chemical composition, that coating is especially hard. But—if you can scratch through the surface of the chromium, you might be able to saw through it, or break the thing open with bolt cutters."

Etna nudged her sister. Elsa leaned in close and listened. Straightening in her chair, she called out, "Chandler dear, come out of the kitchen. We need you, please."

One final bang and Chandler reappeared, the top of his head dusty gray with cobwebs from under the sink. "The only steel wool I found was so rusty it crumbled," he said.

"No worries, dear. Please bring me my valise," Elsa requested. "Be careful, it's old, like me."

Chandler could not tell the two ancient suitcases apart, so he brought them both. Elsa chose one and took out a tiny key she'd been wearing on a string around her neck. The old woman leaned over and unlocked the brass clasps. An aroma of aged leather tinged with Chanel No. 5 wafted up as she picked through fraying pink satin compartments.

"Ah yes. Try this," she said, holding up a metal fingernail file which boasted a bejeweled handle. "QVC special, 1989. Diamond-dusted blade."

Sydney looked up from her notebook. "I remember that. They had a run from the prison system, had to shut it down."

Mike rolled his eyes, pushed back his chair and grunted as he stood up. "Give it here. I'll hack off that lock." Stanley and Chandler went with him. The men stepped back out into the snow. Chandler held the flashlight, Mike filed the chromium down and Stanley sawed the lock off. They paused.

"We're all culpable now," said Stanley, then he turned to Chandler, "But you're in charge of the building."

Chandler nodded. Dreams of a bonus long gone, he bent down to wrestle the valve open. Surprised when it turned easily, he asked, "Anybody have a lighter handy?"

"I do travel with a couple of those," said Mike.

They pushed back the snowy tree branches, descended the cement stairs and approached the octopus. Chandler felt they were about to initiate a sacred rite of Biblical proportions. He opened the old coal furnace and stood back. Mike fished a pearl-handled lighter out of his front pocket and flicked the tiny wheel against the flint. Click, click, click—nothing but a sulfurous whiff of gas. But then the lighter sparked up. All three men smiled at the tiny dancing blue tongue of flame. Stanley turned the knob to HIGH and the flame grew large and yellow. He slammed the door shut.

"How long do you think it'll take to warm this place up?" asked Chandler.

Stanley replied. "It'll take a bit. This is not a well-insulated building. There's lots of air movement, which is a good thing because these stoves are notorious for carbon monoxide poisoning."

Mike swore. "It's always something."

Stanley said, almost gleefully, "But that's not the worst of it. See those arms? They're wrapped in asbestos."

Chandler didn't have long to consider the Angelino's reaction. Mike yelled, "Oh no—we gotta shut it down. That's bad stuff!" and lunged for the control knob.

Stanley grabbed his arm. "This is an emergency!" he yelled.

"ASBESTOS is an emergency!" Mike shouted back and shook off Stanley's grip.

Chandler leaped between him and the furnace, nearly hitting his head on a beam. "How long do you think Miss Elsa and Miss Etna will last in this cold?" he asked.

"They look pretty spry to me," said Mike.

"Hang on Mike," Chandler turned to Stanley. "You seem to know something about this stuff. Are you some kind of chemical engineer? How long before we're poisoned?"

Stanley remained quiet. Mike lunged for the stove again and Chandler tried to hold him back. "C'mon. We need to know."

Stanley said, "Shut up, I'm calculating in my head."

Mike pulled his shirt up over his nose and mouth. The close space was warming.

"We're good," Stanley finally replied. I think we'd have to breathe it for at least three years and a couple of months before major adverse reactions, especially if we crack a window."

Speaking through his shirt Mike said, "You sure about that?"

"Yeah—you just hear a lot of stuff on TV from law firms trying to scare up business. Ha. Scare."

Chandler began to head up the stairs then stopped. "Guys —maybe we should keep the asbestos thing quiet anyway. We don't need anyone panicking. Are you with me?"

Stanley nodded. Mike did not, but he didn't say anything. Upstairs, they found the three women reaching into the rising stream of warmth and dust coughed up by the old grate.

Chandler grabbed Mike by the arm. "Hey, come help me crack open one of the kitchen windows—let's keep some fresh air going.  Besides, what are they going to do, up our gas bill?"

## Chapter 6

Sydney scratched through the block letters. "HEAT? Check." Despite an open window, the temperature was improving. Even Etna soon relinquished her blanket. Stanley and Sydney removed their puffy yellow anoraks to reveal matching pea green pullovers. She looked around at the group and tapped her pen on the page. "Next? Food."

"Yeah!" said Mike. He punched Chandler in the arm. "What's Gran Gran got to eat around here Chan-man? Digging through snow and breaking into gas meters makes me hungry."

Chandler thought of the half a Snickers bar in his car. "We'll have to scrounge around and see what's here. Maybe some leftover cans of something."

"Don't be feeding me any old Twinkies man—those things are radioactive. Make ya glow."

Chandler looked across the room. "Hey Stanley, didn't you have some rations?"

A loud "No" came from the corner by the organ. Stanley was busy unzipping backpacks.

Chandler repeated, "But you said that case I helped you carry in was full of rations."

"Those are special. Sydney and I can't eat the food you do. We're on a special diet. We carry our own food."

"Don't forget the brandy," said Elsa. "There's nothing like a good brandy to warm things up and make everything taste better."

"Great. Brandy, radioactive Twinkies and we get to watch these two eat their 'special' rations," said Mike. "Sounds like a real feast."

Chandler banged back through the kitchen doors. The sounds of rummaging echoed into the dining room.

"I should help him," said Elsa. She joined Chandler in the kitchen. He was pulling out everything he could find. A pile of dusty pots and pans and utensils mounded up on the counter. He made his way toward the frying station, throwing open cupboards and drawers as he went.

"Don't forget to check the lower cabinets," Elsa said.

"Yes ma'am," Chandler replied through clinched teeth, as he bent down.

"We'll be alright, young man,"

"Oh yes we will, and so will that Stanley when he meets this frying pan."

Elsa laughed. "Oh, he is a case. And his poor wife. What a match."

Chandler opened a tall narrow cabinet beside the stove and began to laugh with her. "They match alright. When I saw their green... hey! Green beans! Look here Miss Elsa! Green beans. Large economy size." He lifted up a three-pound can, its previously white label crusted with greasy gray dust. "Let's see what Mike thinks about this." He stooped back down. "This cabinet's really deep." Reaching all the way back, his fingers discovered two glass mason jars and a tall square black tin.

"Tell Sydney we have something to add to the food list," he

said, holding up one of the jars. "Somebody around here did some canning. Peaches? I think? They look a little dark."

Elsa said, "Oh yes. Peaches, I'm sure. How is the lid?"

He passed her the jar. She tested the lid with her finger, no movement. She held the jar up, sniffed it and peered closely at the dark gold contents. "I don't see any bubbles, I'm sure these are good."

"Look here Miss Elsa," he placed the tall tin on the countertop. The lid was so tight he had to pry it off with a knife. Suddenly it popped up and off. "Corn meal! Yes!" He tipped the can slightly and they could see that the pale, yellow meal, while coarse, was dry and good. "No mice here."

Miss Elsa clapped her hands. "Praises be."

"We can make cornmeal mush. My grandmother Nonnie taught me that one a long time ago."

"Good woman," said Elsa. "And we have peach topping. Can you get this old stove going?"

"I'll need Mike's lighter, but yes, I think so. Cornmeal mush with peach topping. That might be pretty good."

Elsa nodded, "with brandy."

"And green beans."

"Who needs 'rations'?"

The kitchen conspirators returned to the dining room. While Mike still poked at one of the grates, Sydney and Stanley rattled around in their corner, opening foil ration bags that crackled with every move. Neither one made any attempt to dampen the noise.

Etna remained seated at the table, eyes closed, breathing in a light steady rhythm.

"Hey Mike, let me borrow your lighter again," said Chandler.

"Sure. What for?"

"It's time to cook your feast."

"Radiated Twinkies?"

"Nope. How about some green beans, well-aged?"

Mike made a face. "Bettern' nuthin'." He tossed the pearl-handled lighter to Chandler.

Elsa joined Etna at the table. "We're in good hands Ettie. We found cornmeal."

Mike shook his head and pulled a table over the grate, raising more dust. Chandler returned to the kitchen and rolled up his sleeves. It took a few minutes to finesse the old stove. Just when he had managed to light the pilot light, he heard a knock on the door.

## Chapter 7

Chandler heard the knock again. Definitely the back door, and a little louder this time. *Who now?* He wiped corn-meal-dusted hands on the front of his jeans and cracked open the door. A wave of cold air blew in and extinguished the pilot light.

Two small forms stood shivering, huddled together. Chandler pushed the door open, "Come in, come in! What are you doing out here?!" He pulled them in as fast as he could and slammed the door.

The person who had taken his hand pulled back a purple sweatshirt hood to reveal a brown-skinned woman. Very short black hair, shaved close on one side, stood straight up and out all over her head. Her companion, not quite as tall, stood shivering as if in shock. All Chandler could see were skinny legs under a giant, pink fur-trimmed parka. "Thank you so much, sir. We were traveling here and saw the light, we had to stop, our plane had to make a landing in Amarillo, but we must keep going to New York City. We will not be staying long here, we just need to rest for a little while." The woman's thick accent was hard to understand. Chandler wondered if she might be from Mexico. He couldn't quite place it.

"Yes ma'am! Nobody needs to be driving right now. This

restaurant is closed, but we have heat and water and just a little food." The woman grabbed his hand.

"Thank you, sir. Thank you so much. We are so very tired. We left Memphis this morning, and I am the one doing all the driving. My niece is not driving yet."

"Your niece?"

"Yes, this is AngelBaby."

As if on cue, the girl pulled back the fur-trimmed hood and Chandler beheld one of the most exquisite faces he could ever remember seeing. Feathery eyebrows arched over large brown, almond-shaped eyes. Full lips commanded attention under a delicate nose. A tiny mole perched below one eye oversaw a smattering of ginger freckles lightly sprinkled across perfect café-au lait skin.

He instantly thought of Sherr and missed her all the more.

"Welcome Angel ... uh ... baby. And... ?"

"My name is Rosalinda. You may call me Rosie. That is my nickname."

"Yes, Rosie, of course, and AngelBaby. Why did you come to the back door?"

"We went to the front door first and knocked and knocked but no one answered, but we could see the people inside and the lights."

Chandler gritted his teeth. Had the first round of guests ignored them? "Well, I'm glad you came back here and tried again."

"We had no choice. We are almost out of fuel. We had to wait a very long time to get off the highway and, and..." Rosie choked back a sob. AngelBaby wrapped her arms around her aunt. Chandler wanted to scoop them both up into a hug, but thought better of it.

"You're here now. It's OK. Let me introduce you to the others."

Rosie patted the hair down on top of her head but it sprang back up. She took AngelBaby's face in her hands and examined for any defects. "OK darling, let's go and meet them now."

Chandler was tempted to go for grand—swing open the scarred red double doors with a flourish and announce: *And now, Ladies and Gentlemennnn, Rosalinda and her niece An- gelba-...* But no. Just let them in and hope for peace. He held open the door and ushered the two newcomers into the dining room. Stanley and Sydney remained in their corner, and the sisters at the table. Mike had finally abandoned the grate. He was trying to pry open an old radio with a rusty screwdriver.

Chandler nudged Rosie and AngelBaby toward the sisters. "Miss Elsa, Miss Etna, we have some new guests." Etna seemed to still be sleeping but Elsa reached out her hand in welcome. "Come in from the snow, fellow travelers, come in, come in— where did you come from?"

"They had to come around by the back door—didn't any- one hear them knock?"

Mike looked up from his pile of junk and grunted, "Now who?" Then he saw AngelBaby and stood up, straightening his shirt tail.

Rosie instantly approached him dragging AngelBaby by the arm. "My name is Rosie. We have been traveling for a long time now from the Philippines, on our way to New York City. This is my niece, AngelBaby. She is going to be featured on a TV special for New Year's Eve." She thrust her forward, "Sing for them Angel."

The girl shook her arm free. "Auntie Rosie, I'm so tired, please can I sing later? We just got here." Chandler was shocked to hear a very American accent. Sounding nothing like Rosie, she could have been from Hawaii or LA or Chicago. Philippines? *OK. Would not have guessed.*

"That's a very long way," said Elsa.

Stanley and Sydney rejoined the group. "Philippines! My dad was stationed at Subic Bay Naval Base."

Stanley rolled his eyes. "Don't get her started talking about her dad."

In the growing clatter of conversation, AngelBaby slipped past her aunt to the elderly sisters' table. Elsa's eyes lit up and she received AngelBaby with glee. Rosie continued to engage with Mike until he passed her off on Sydney to talk about the Navy and Subic Bay and who was where when Mt. Pinatubo blew up. Grabbing Chandler by the arm, Mike said, "Chandler needs my help in the kitchen now." He practically pushed the younger man through the doors.

"We gotta turn that sign off man. It's getting crowded in here."

"Did you hear them knocking on the front door?"

"No. I swear I didn't."

Chandler turned to the can of green beans. "Well, if anyone else knocks, we've got to let them in. They drove all the way from Memphis today. Rosie said they got stuck on the interstate for hours and were almost out of fuel. If there are more people out there, they might freeze. We have to let them in."

Mike nodded. "OK man, you're right."

Everything was quiet for a few moments, then the lights went out.

## Chapter 8

A split second of silence exploded into shouts from the dining room.

"Hey!"

"You said we had lights!"

"Chandler?" Elsa's voice quavered.

"Be right there! We're looking for candles," shouted Chandler. "Everybody stay where you are." He pulled out his phone and tapped open the flashlight app. Hadn't he seen candles earlier?

"That'll use up your battery fast, man."

"I know there are some candles around here."

"I saw some old kerosene lamps on a shelf," Mike nodded toward the dining room, his face looking more pirate-like than ever in the shadows.

The two returned to find AngelBaby and Rosie shining their cellphone lights as well. Etna took no notice of anything, and Elsa turned to Chandler. He sensed her unspoken directive to solve the problem but was at a loss.

Rustling noises from the corner suddenly resulted in two bright white beams glaring across the room. Sydney and Stanley emerged crowned with headlamps. They looked like matching miners. The bright LED beams made it difficult to look them in the face. "These will go for hours," boasted Stanley. "I charged them all the way up before we left." Squinting, Elsa raised her hand to shade her eyes.

"How about let's try just one for now?" said Chandler. "We might need the other one later, if you're willing to share."

"Of course, of course. Can't have people falling over each other." Stanley turned his lamp off.

"We can save the cellphones then." Sydney said. AngelBaby, Rosie and Chandler shut down their lights. Then Sydney took her headlamp off and handed it to Chandler. "You're tall. Point this thing at the ceiling."

He followed her instructions and placed it high on a shelf. Hanging decorations cast huge, strange shadows, but the reflected glow off the old, yellowed ceiling was much easier on the eyes than the stark white headlamp blast.

Elsa relaxed her salute. "Thank you. Now, what about that cornmeal mush?" the elderly woman asked Chandler.

"Well, the pilot light went out. Maybe somebody can help me get that gas stove going again. Stanley? And bring your lamp."

AngelBaby began tugging on Rosie's arm and whispered something in her ear. "Elvis," said Rosie. "Elvis is in the car. We have to get him out. It is too cold for him and he will freeze."

"Elvis is dead," said Mike.

"No, no!" cried AngelBaby, "Elvis is my dog. I got him in Memphis. Please Mister, will you help us get him out of the car? I can't leave him out there to die."

Mike pushed up from the table with a sigh. "OK, let's go get Elvis." Rosie gave him a big smile and the car keys to their rental vehicle.

"We are driving the big blue van, it's just there." She

motioned with her lips, almost like blowing a kiss. "It's the blue one. And of course we have our bags in there as well. Can you kindly please help us?"

Mike muttered something under his breath while Chandler and Stanley and Sydney went to figure out the stove.

The wind had begun to grow louder, but everyone *really* noticed it when Mike stomped out to rescue Elvis the dog. The blue van was the only vehicle in the parking lot not completely covered up. No one would have guessed the snow mounds hid a Bentley, a Tesla, a VW and his Harley. Mike tried not to think about what might be happening to its cylinders.

A frantic little brown and white furry face hopped up and down in the back seat of the van. Mike could see it bark, but barely hear anything above the wind. "Oh, I should put you out of all our misery now." It would be easy—open the door, toss the dog and let it fend for itself. But then he thought of AngelBaby and those big brown pleading eyes.

The side door swung open and he was hit by the smell of dog. Elvis immediately jumped into his arms and began licking his face. "Stop it you dumb dog!" Once again, he was tempted to toss it into the woods. But instead, Mike made his way through the snow, up the front stairs, across the porch to the front door, while holding the squirming animal at arm's length. He threw Elvis into Gran Gran's. Not stopping to watch the joyful reunion with AngelBaby, Mike waded back through the snow and gathered up as much as he could carry out of the van in one trip: a couple of big bright yellow roller bags, another coat and a purple plastic tub with a lid. Sliding the door, and hearing the latch click shut, he hauled it all back to the restaurant and dumped it in a dripping heap beside the front door.

"Thank you, thank you so much! I can never thank you enough!" said Rosie. AngelBaby was busy with Elvis, who seemed no worse for the wear. Mike grunted, and brought clasped hands close to his mouth, blowing on them.

"Brandy?" Elsa held up a silver flask.

"Yes ma'am, thank you so much."

The swig warmed him all the way down.

*****

Sydney and Stanley fussed at each other and the stove while Chandler tried to remember how his grandmother made mush. The water from the tap felt icy cold but *at least we have water.* He heard a pop then smelled gas.

"Light 'er up!" He yelled, running over to click Mike's lighter and ignite the stove.

"Just like hot-wiring a car," boasted Stanley. "First you take the..."

"I knew you could do it." Sydney punched him on the arm. "Ow!"

Chandler emptied the green beans into one saucepan and put another saucepan of water on to heat. He added cold water into his bowl of dried cornmeal and stirred it into paste. Once the water began to boil, he began stirring in the cold cornmeal paste. "No lumps!" he said. "If it comes out lumpy, I did something wrong."

"Looks like you know what you're doing," said Stanley. "Were you in the Navy, Cookie?" Sydney punched his arm.

"Ow!"

"Nope, just worked my way through school in a restaurant a whole lot like this one," Chandler replied.

"Not engineering school." said Stanley. Sydney punched his arm again. "Ow, *stop* it!"

"Nope," the younger man began to grin.

"Business school?" asked Sydney.

"Not me!" Chandler laughed.

"Culinary school then," she said.

"Nope. You won't guess, so I'll tell you. Seminary."

Chandler knew exactly what would happen next. Sydney and Stanley who had just begun to seem a little human suddenly went quiet.

"It's OK, I'm a regular dude. Go back to thinking of me as a cook," he laughed.

The couple mumbled a few words and edged back into the dining room.

*Ah Sherr, if you could see your amazing husband now.* He looked at his cellphone just in case there might be a message but no. *Busy with your mom, I'm sure.* He took a moment to send a quick text.

**Miss u sweetheart gotta save this battery lights out**

## *Chapter 9*

Chandler plated up cornmeal mush, swimming with warm peaches and a side of green beans. *Looks OK.* Pulling a fork from the pile of utensils, he pushed his way through the double doors and presented the steaming plate to Elsa with a flourish. "Madam." He made a little bow, as if she was the favored patron of an elegant establishment.

Elsa sat up straight and tall and gave him a gracious nod. "Thank you, kind sir," She took a small bite. "That is mighty fine." It could have been plum pudding on a dainty silver spoon.

Mike rolled his eyes but joined Chandler in the kitchen to plate up and deliver portions to Etna, Rosie and AngelBaby. Once the "womenfolk" (as he called them) were settled, he topped up his plate with green beans, peaches and a big yellow mound of mush. Chandler kept quiet. There was plenty. Grabbing his plate, he returned to the dining room to find Stanley and Sydney at the table, each with their own ration tin, foil bag and water bottle. They scooted one more table across the old wooden floor so all could gather around.

"Now it's starting to feel like Christmas," said Chandler. "And no one has to sit at the kid's table."

"Would you say Grace, dear?" said Elsa. "Sydney told us you are a man of the cloth."

Chandler looked around. They were all quiet. "Ummm, of course." Rosie and AngelBaby crossed themselves.

"Dear Jesus. Thank you for bringing us all out of that terrible storm outside. Thank you for giving us this food. Please help us return to our families in safety. Amen." He lifted his head. "Bon appetit! Or as my wife would say, '*Buen Provecho!*'"

Mike wasted no time shoveling in mouthfuls. "This is alright man. When you said green beans, that's all I thought we'd get."

Elsa helped Etna adjust a scarf around her neck to get it out of the way. The smell of food seemed to revive her and she ate slowly, displaying the elegant manners of days long gone by. As he took a bite of the corn mush Chandler wished for salt, and glanced over at Rosie and AngelBaby. Their green beans were gone. The yellow mush remained. AngelBaby pushed her spoon through it whispering something in dialect to her aunt.

"I'm sorry there's no salt," said Chandler to Rosie. "It would make the corn mush taste better."

Rosie said, "It's OK, we are not used to eating this at home."

AngelBaby broke in, "It's pig food." Rosie jerked the girl's shoulder hard and said something no one could understand.

"I'm sorry," said AngelBaby, "I don't mean to offend you. I've watched *Little House on the Prairie*, so I know you eat this. But in the Philippines, corn meal is what we feed to pigs."

"I'm no pig," growled Mike with his mouth full.

Chandler laughed. "Well you are missing out. Too bad my wife is not here, she could make you some awesome cornmeal fritters. *Suru*-somethings, I never could say it right."

Elsa patted AngelBaby's other shoulder. "Young lady, when

you travel to someone else's country sometimes you have to try new things."

"Do you have any rice?" AngelBaby asked Chandler, ignoring another tug from Auntie Rosie.

"My dad said a meal in the Philippines was not a meal unless you had rice," offered up Sydney. Rosie and AngelBaby nodded in agreement. Chandler resisted the temptation to ask Sydney if they had any rice stowed in their ration stash.

He said, "I'm sorry. I didn't see any rice in the kitchen. I think we were pretty lucky to find this. Why don't you try just a little bite? It's good with the peach topping."

"And if you don't want it, I'll finish yours," said Mike.

"We have to eat it, darling," said Rosie. "Let us just give it a try." She put a tiny crumb on the end of her fork, slathered it in peach-syrup and squinting her eyes placed it on the very tip of her tongue. "It's not bad. Try to pretend it's *halo-halo*," she said. AngelBaby, imagining one of her favorite Filipino treats, followed suit. Elsa smiled.

"So, does anybody have a read on the weather?" asked Chandler.

"Forecast says this is supposed to last a couple of days," replied Stanley looking up from his cellphone.

"It's a real Alberta Clipper," added Sydney. "My dad ..."

"No one cares about your dad," interrupted Stanley.

"... was a weatherman after he retired from the Navy." Sydney glared at her husband with stormy blue eyes then turned back to the group. "Did you know that North America has the most volatile weather of any continent in the world?"

"Makes sense to me," said Mike. "Try a little motorcycle touring. You'll find out pretty quick."

"Our plane had to take an emergency landing in Amarillo," said Rosie. She rolled her R's beautifully. "Because of the storm they said they could not continue to fly. But we had to find a way to go to New York. Thanks to God we were able to rent a car and keep traveling."

"You've been on the road nonstop since Amarillo?" Mike asked. "That's impressive." He nodded with respect.

AngelBaby said, "We made a stop in Memphis. We have a cousin there, and they gave me Elvis." Upon hearing his name, a little brown and white furry face popped up from her lap. She gave him a bite of mush.

"So, we need to think about camping here for a bit," said Chandler.

"No one will come looking for us," said Elsa. "But they might come looking for some of you."

Stanley and Sydney glanced at each other, then away. "Not us," said Sydney. "Our boys are out west and think we're doing the normal holiday thing. They probably figure we're already at the casino ..."

Stanley broke in, "And we already would have been there if SOMEONE hadn't gotten us off to such a late start." Sydney ignored him.

"No one's looking for me either," said Mike. "I was gonna surprise my mom for Christmas. She thinks I'm headed for New Orleans. Shoulda stuck with that plan."

"The Angelino brothers only care about getting their report on this place a couple of days after Christmas," said Chandler. "And I'm going to have an interesting time telling them what happened."

"We are just stopping here for tonight only. We will leave early in the morning for New York City," Rosie announced.

Chandler shook his head. "You're low on fuel."

"We will stop at the next station."

Mike shook his head. "First you'll have to dig out and then hope something's open—not gonna happen."

Rosie began to protest, but Chandler interrupted. "What's this TV thing in New York?" he asked.

"I made a TikTok video," said AngelBaby.

"A video about a clock?" said Elsa, "That is very interesting for a girl your age."

AngelBaby looked at her aunt, and Rosie produced her cellphone. "But you have to sing it for them so they can really understand, darling."

"Can we do it tomorrow? I'm really tired."

Chandler broke in, "I think we need something to look forward to tomorrow—we may be here awhile. How about we settle in for the night?" AngelBaby shot a look of gratitude his way and he winked.

Elsa said to Etna, "Young people are so imaginative these days, Ettie. There's going to be something about a clock to-morrow."

"Dust."

Rosie and her niece helped Chandler clear the table.

"I'll take care of these dishes," said Chandler. "Let's see about beds."

The elderly sisters elected to stay at the table. "We sleep sitting up in our armchairs half the time anyway," said Elsa.

The Stanley and Sydney corner was mostly quiet except for

the slap of playing cards and cutting remarks from a contentious game of blackjack.

Chandler located a grate across the room from the blackjack. He pushed a couple of chairs and a table into a bit of an enclosure to provide Rosie and AngelBaby a bit of warmth and privacy.

"You and I can bunk in the kitchen," he said to Mike.

Everyone was almost settled when they heard a chair scrape across the floor followed by Elsa's slow steps. She made the rounds with her flask.

"Just a little nip to help you sleep."

Stanley said, "No thanks," but Sydney took some, as did Rosie.

AngelBaby looked hopeful, but her aunt said, "No, it will make your voice raspy, darling."

Mike and Chandler flipped a coin over who got the counter. Mike won. He slung Rosie's extra coat over his legs. Chandler heated up some water on the stove and gave the dishes a rinse. There was no soap. Propping his feet up on a chair, he pulled his coat around him. It was really just a big fleecy sweatshirt Sherr had brought home a few weeks ago. He pulled it close, wishing for his wife.

*Silent night... I hope.*

## Chapter 10

"Mmmm, yes darling, I'd love another cup of coffee." Tousled, Early Morning Sherr uncurled from the couch and slipped across their apartment to the little galley kitchen. It was not far but Chandler loved every stretch of those long legs.

Suddenly he heard urgent, high-pitched yapping. *Who let a dog in? We don't have a dog ...* Visions of Sherr melted into the cold stiff reality of a long night in a kitchen chair. Elvis needed out.

Mike still snored, oblivious on the counter. Rubbing his eyes, Chandler found Rosie and AngelBaby trying to open the front door.

"We're snowed in," came Stanley's muffled voice from the corner.

Etna and Elsa were not to be found, but were probably in the Ladies room. Chandler's early morning brain was not ready to process anything. He yawned and wished for coffee.

"Try the window," said Sydney. She pushed up and out from her nest of blankets. "I'm sure the snow has drifted up against the building. Put him out through the window. He'll come back, I promise."

"He'll drown!" cried AngelBaby.

"Wait," said Chandler, beginning to wake up. "Let's try the back door first—maybe it hasn't drifted so much on that side."

A teary AngelBaby nodded and handed squirming Elvis to Chandler. She followed him to the kitchen, and watched as Chandler wrestled the back door open and let the little dog out. He promptly sank, AngelBaby screamed, but then Elvis found footing. They could barely see his little brown and white head bob along. Snow still fell at a steady pace, though the wind had died down a little.

Chandler laughed. "Poor little guy."

Within moments Elvis returned. AngelBaby grabbed him and wrapped him up in her blanket until all you could see was the tip of his nose. Chandler followed them back into the dining area. Mike had slept through the entire incident.

"Well, Elvis is good. I sure could use some coffee." Chandler said.

"There's coffee?" Sydney looked hopeful.

"No, I was just dreaming that my wife Sherr was getting me a second cup. Her folks send us coffee from Puerto Rico. Then I heard this little dog." He glanced at AngelBaby. Elvis was happy in her arms.

"We grow delicious coffee beans in the Philippines," said Rosie. "But I did not bring any here with me."

"Too bad," said Chandler and Sydney, almost at the same time.

Elsa and Etna returned. Bright, brushed and freshly powdered, they looked ready for a holiday brunch out with the girls. "Did someone say coffee? We used to put chicory in our coffee. That was good, wasn't it, Ettie dear?"

Etna surprised everyone by saying, "Chicory," and smiled.

"What is this chicory?" asked Rosie.

"It is something Papa picked up from his customers in New Orleans—it's from a flower."

"Ah, yes. We also have so many edible flowers in the Philippines," said Rosie.

"I think it's the root of the plant, but the flowers are a very pretty blue color," explained Elsa.

Sydney said, "My dad used to tell a story about a Filipino ambassador to the White House who asked the President if he could say 'grace' for the meal in his own language. He used to tell it so funny. 'Oh Lord, we thank you for this meal, and nobody eat the flowers!' He wanted to make sure his entourage was up on what not to do."

Rosie laughed. "And when the American president visited the Philippines, they probably told him to make sure to eat the flowers."

"What's there to eat?" Mike came banging through the kitchen doors, black bushy hair standing on end, pink and yellow polka-dot coat wrapped around his shoulders.

"No flowers," said Chandler.

"Huh?"

Sydney went back to the corner and pushed the blanket off the top of Stanley's head.

"Hey,"

"Shut up, I'm sleeping,"

"No you're not," she said.

"Go away."

Sydney pushed passed her husband and grabbed one of the plastic cases. At the sound of opening clasps, Stanley's balding head popped up.

"What are you doing?"

"Making breakfast," she replied as she pulled out a set of green foil packets.

"Oh. OK." Stanley disappeared back under the blanket.

Sydney beckoned to Chandler. She handed him the packets. He saw "PROTEIN" displayed prominently on the label.

"It's better if you use hot water," she said, "And even then…"

Stanley's head popped back up. "What are you doing? Those are our rations!"

"Shut up, Stanley. There's no coffee. I'm sharing."

Stanley stood up. Blankets fell to the floor, revealing skinny legs and boxer shorts. He hastily pulled a blanket around him. "We need that. We can't eat their food."

"They don't have food Stanley, and I am not going to eat in front of them."

"Thank you, ma'am," said Chandler as he pushed Mike back to the kitchen. He could still hear Stanley complaining.

"Well, now we know someone in the family has a heart," said Mike.

Chandler opened one of the packets and put it up to his nose, which twitched at a faint whiff of seaweed. "Maybe."

He read the instructions, heated some water and poured in the powder. "Contents ready when reach pudding consistency."

With stirring, the brew bubbled into a smooth greenish brown goo just beyond paste, but not quite Cream of Wheat. He ladled it into bowls. Mike took a bite, made a face, then went to deliver.

Nobody said much, but everyone did their best to swallow and smile. Stanley continued to pout in the corner. Sydney ate each bite with enthusiastic overkill. "We're participating in a study," she said. "Nobody has access to this stuff yet, but when it hits the market just wait." Everyone sipped slowly from their spoons.

"Dust," mumbled Etna.

"No, actually it's algae-based protein," replied Sydney. "Super-high in anti-oxidants."

"I remember one of those end-of-the-world movies from the Seventies," interrupted Mike. "They were eating stuff just like this."

Rosie said, "That movie came to the Philippines when I was a little girl. *Soylent Green.* My older brothers used to tell me if I was bad they would send me to the food factory."

A burst of laughter came from Stanley, "See what you get for being friendly, Sydney? They just accused us of cannibalism."

"Shut up, Stanley. I remember the movie. This is algae, people."

"And don't forget the Donner party," Stanley added.

Elsa and Etna glanced at each other in confusion. Angel-Baby returned her spoon to the bowl. She lowered it into her lap. Elvis sniffed but did not partake.

"*Really* Stanley?" said his wife. She shook her head and turned to the group. "Honestly, I think he's on the spectrum."

Stanley yelled, "I heard that!"

"Good!" his wife shouted back.

Chandler stood up and tapped his fork on his bowl. "Uh— hey everybody, it's Christmas Eve."

Mike scraped his spoon against the bowl, "Not that bad once you get into it a little."

Chandler gathered up the bowls. "Well, later today, when

we're hungry, I am sure we will all appreciate this even more. "Sydney, thank you for sharing. That was very kind of you."

Stanley mocked him. "Thank you for sharing, thank you for sharing. We'll all be hungry soon."

Back in the kitchen Mike said, "You know, we might need a gun."

"What do you mean? For Stanley?" replied Chandler, "No way. Not me."

"No. I bet there's some turkey around, probably even deer. We could be stuck here awhile."

"We'll get out of here before too long," said Chandler.

"Maybe, maybe not."

"Besides, who has a gun? Do you have a gun?"

Mike said, "I bet Stanley does. Those old ladies might even have one in their car."

The thought of killing and butchering anything turned Chandler's stomach. Algae protein sounded better. He pulled out his phone. Not much battery left.

**Sherr miss u so much pray 4 us**

He was surprised by an immediate reply.

**Mom gone**

A great weight rose up in Chandler's gut. He frantically typed

**no no Sherr so sorry I'm not with u**

But the battery, already red, expired and the screen went dark. Chandler slowly sank back into the chair he'd slept in and laid his head on the table.

"Bad news?" said Mike.

"Sherr's mom didn't make it." Saying it out loud made it feel too real.

"Oh man. I'm sorry."

"It's Christmas Eve. Why couldn't she have just lasted even for a couple more days? And why didn't I go with her? I should have never let Sherr go home by herself." Chandler slammed the table. Blinded by tears, he headed for the back door and shoved it open.

Mike handed the young man his hat. "Don't be long man, it's cold."

Chandler charged out into the storm, not paying attention to the instant cold wet of snow up around and past his knees then thighs. The wind had picked up again. If he had not been so cold and distraught, the sight of so much snow falling and blowing around against the backdrop of tall evergreens might have been beautiful.

*God! No! You cannot do this to Sherr! And you cannot do this to me—not again! I learned those lessons already. You know I did.* The clouded heavens only released more snow. Chandler began to shiver. *I can't go back in there.* Silence. *I need to be with Sherr! Now!* The imperative glanced off the gloomy heavens and bounced back on him. *Please?* He shut his eyes tight hoping to find himself transported to the Palacio's farm. It only grew colder. He opened his eyes. All he could see was the backside of Gran Gran's and the deep snow trampled by his rant. He could barely make out the back door. *Really? This is not fair in any way. I should have gone with her. Why didn't you make me change my mind and go with her?* All he heard was wind skimming through tree branches. Finally, realizing he could not feel his toes, Chandler stumbled back through the snow. Mike was no longer in the kitchen, but his spare pair of baggy black sweats and a t-shirt sat on Chandler's chair. He put them on.

In the dining area, Mike cleared his throat. "Uhh. Hey everybody. Chan's wife just lost her mom."

Everyone grew silent. Rosie crossed herself, touching the tip of her thumb to her lower lip as she finished. AngelBaby copied her.

Elsa bowed her head and placed her arm around her sister. "Poor dear," she said. "Every time you lose someone you love, it feels like the first time." Etna nodded slowly.

Chandler pushed through the kitchen doors. Mike nodded at him. "I told them."

Chandler could barely look at the travelers. They no longer saw a confident young man playing the host. "I'd ... I'd like to pray for Sherr and her family." His voice sounded thin and raspy. "Would you guys be OK with that?"

The guests seemed unsure for a moment.

Then Mike put his hand on Chandler's shoulder. Rosie took Mike's hand. AngelBaby took her aunt's hand. Sydney took Etna's papery thin hand in her own and glanced at the corner. Stanley shook his head, no. Sydney closed the circle, taking Chandler's left hand in her own. She looked down. In one hand she held a cool, blue-white veiny claw. The other was lost in the trembling clasp of a golden-brown young man.

"Oh God. I praise you. How can I be so far away from Sherr when she needs me? And how can she be feeling right now losing her mother? Please bless them, please help them. And Lord, God, I believe you care. I know you do. That's why we even have Christmas—because you care. But this hurts. Thank you for these friends here today. Please bless them. Please bless their families wherever they are, and please bring us through this horrible storm. And please forgive me. And help Sherr to forgive me for not being with her today. In the name of your son Jesus, Amen."

"Amen," echoed Elsa. Rosie and AngelBaby and Mike crossed themselves. A muffled grunt came from the corner.

*****

As the day passed, the storm grew stronger than ever, rejuvenated by a wave of moisture off the coast. Most were quiet. The sisters napped and nipped brandy. Stanley and Sydney resumed their contentious card game. Their fellow travelers ignored the occasional outburst from the corner. AngelBaby and Rosie flipped through issues of *People* magazine, did their nails and made a game out of asking Mike to help them let Elvis in and out. Mike pretended to be annoyed and tinkered with the radio he had reduced to a pile of pieces. Chandler stayed to himself, searching for more food while he cleaned up the kitchen.

The short afternoon began to darken, Elsa awoke and said, "What about that clock presentation? Miss Rosie? Baby Angel?"

Rosie looked at her niece. "It's time now. You need to practice." Any hopes to refuel and head north lay buried in the parking lot.

AngelBaby nodded. "OK Auntie. Do you have the music?"

"I have just a little battery left." Rosie waved her cellphone toward the Ladies room. "Go get ready. Full costume."

Her niece zipped up one of the yellow roller bags and headed down the hall. A full 45 minutes later she returned.

AngelBaby left as a schoolgirl in two long braids that hung down the back of a baggy pink sweatshirt over black leggings. They did not recognize what returned.

Mike whistled under his breath, "Now that's what I call 'loaded for bear.'"

Gingery freckles were concealed by artful, if heavy makeup that shaded every feature for emphasis—especially the large brown eyes now fringed by eyelashes so long and thick they resembled plumes. Her hair, subjected to a severe center part, cascaded in long sausage curls down to the back of her knees just below hot-pink thigh-high boots. A swath of smooth brown skin was visible from boot-top to high hemline of shiny red pleated vinyl and topped off by a fur-trimmed, skin-tight sequined pink long-sleeved "sweater" buttoned to the neck that ended just below her sternum.

"My microphone is out of battery," she waved a tiny headset at her aunt.

"It's OK. The cellphone is not that loud. Just sing."

Elsa clapped her hands. "My, how glamorous! This is a real show! When you get a little taller you can be a Rockette!"

Rosie had cleared space beside their sleeping area. She moved to the side so AngelBaby could take center stage. "Wait, wait just one moment. We need the judges." Rosie pointed to Stanley, "You be Jay."

"Jay who?"

"Leno of course. Please sit over there at that table." She pointed to Mike. "And you, sir..."

"Yes ma'am?"

"You will be Simon, please."

"Simon?"

"Simon Cowell of course. Thank you."

Mike obediently took a seat beside Jay.

"We need one more judge," she looked at Chandler who had just come in from the kitchen. He shook his head no. The sisters were not going to move.

"Sydney?"

"Yes?"

"You will be Jennifer Lopez. OK, please?"

"I'll try."

Stanley snickered and she gave him a dirty look. "Shut up, Stanley."

"Jay," he replied. Sydney rolled her eyes.

Rosie stepped out to the center of the room. "Presenting, from Tacloban, Philippines, home of the most beautiful women in the world, including four Miss Universes ... ANGELBABY!"

She dropped back to the side and hit Play. AngelBaby stood, head bowed. A low tone emitted from the cellphone and she began to moan, raising her head and fluttering eyelash plumes at the audience. A steady beat, backed by a double bass, throbbed out and broke into a syncopation that AngelBaby matched—first with her body and then with an unexpectedly powerful voice that rang and echoed off all the hard wooden surfaces, no mic needed.

Etna put her hands over her ears. Eyes closed, the tiny girl belted out a string of lyrics—something about 'my lover this' and 'I like this and this and this' all the while contorting her body and whipping her hair around like a whirling dervish.

She never lost beat, her voice never broke, and no one could take their eyes off her. It was done in precisely 1 minute and 36 seconds.

They sat in shock.

AngelBaby moved back to her aunt's side and picked up Elvis.

"Judges?" commanded Rosie.

"Wow," said Mike. "That's all I can say. Wow." He slowly clapped his hands.

"Jay?"

"Umm." Stanley glanced at Sydney who looked stunned. "That was um, quite a performance. Yes, very precise."

Rosie looked at Sydney, "And Miss Lopez, what do you have to say about my niece's performance?"

"Who in the world taught her to do that?" demanded Sydney.

"Someone in our family," said Rosie. "They were formerly a coach for ..."

Sydney interrupted her, glaring straight at AngelBaby. "Young lady, I hope you know there are other ways to make a living—like with your brain." She stood with a humph and returned to her corner.

Stanley said, "Oh don't mind her. She gets mad when I turn on the Dallas Cowboy Cheerleaders."

"I heard that, Stanley."

Rosie whispered something and AngelBaby left for the bathroom.

Then Rosie stood and faced the group. "That girl is the hope of Tacloban. Her mother could have been a famous singer, but she was killed in Typhoon Yolanda when AngelBaby was just a tiny child." Rosie's voice rose. "This girl will be better than Vilma Santos, Nora Aunor and Sharon Cuneta combined. Her TikTok video opened a very important door. Do you know what it means for her to be featured on the New Year's show?" Her voice continued to rise and she pinpointed Sydney. "Did your father ever tell you about the other side of life at Subic Bay? Where families sold their daughters to U.S. servicemen? This is nothing. And this is everything. DO NOT give Angel-Baby any reason to doubt her talent or her opportunity."

Chandler did not know what to say. AngelBaby's exotic performance was over the top, but not far from high school cheerleader dance routines in his neighborhood. And she could definitely sing.

Mike and Stanley backed away from the judge's seats while Rosie, thin-lipped, put away the chairs with exaggerated care. No one offered to help. All they could hear beyond her scraping and thumping was the whine of the wind whipping around the corners.

Chandler suddenly wondered how long the old roof would stand up to the high winds and heavy snow. Under all the décor it was hard to see if the ceiling was sagging anywhere.

After a long time, Elsa spoke up. "Back in my day, we had a young protégé in our family," she said.

"You understand me then," said Rosie.

Elsa nodded and patted her sister's arm. She did not respond. Elsa said, "My sister Ettie showed such talent as a little girl that a music teacher came over from the university forty miles away every week to teach her piano and organ." Etna looked up at her sister. Elsa patted her arm again. "By the age of twelve, she played for the choir and all the Sunday services. My sister was the youngest paid member on the church staff." No one replied. Elsa nodded toward Stanley and Sydney's corner. "There is an organ over there Ettie, would you like to play?"

Mike groaned.

AngelBaby, face freshly scrubbed, returned as a kid in a sweatshirt.

## *Chapter 11*

"This is ridiculous," grumbled Stanley. "We need to focus on getting out of here before we run out of rations." He gave Sydney the evil eye.

"Shut up, Stanley. We can't move. Rescue teams can't move. We just have to wait. A little distraction *might* keep us from killing each other in the meantime. Don't forget the Donner party."

Muttering under his breath, Stanley helped Sydney move the matching backpacks, anoraks and blankets, neatly rolled up in bungee cord cocoons, away from the pump organ. All offers to help were refused. Within a few minutes the gear was stacked in a pyramid, ration cases covered up, in the corner closest to the front door.

"It'll be cold here tonight," Stanley grumbled.

"Shut up, Stanley, we can move back over by the grate later."

Sydney turned to Elsa and Etna, "We're ready."

Elsa took her sister by the hand and led her to the ancient instrument. AngelBaby followed close behind.

"Dust," Etna shook her head.

AngelBaby immediately raced to her side and tried to wipe off the old instrument with her sleeve. Mike handed AngelBaby a red bandanna from his back pocket. She used it for a moment, then ran to the kitchen and rinsed it out. Once damp, the faded cotton cloth removed most of the film. Chandler pulled out the bench and seated the frail woman. Elsa placed her sister's hands on the keyboard.

"Put your feet on the pedals, dear."

Etna placed her feet on the old pump pedals and began to press them. This raised more dust, but she said nothing.

"Please play for us," said AngelBaby. "How about a Christmas song?"

Etna continued to pump the pedals. Then slowly, she moved her hands. Notes wheezed out as she pressed keys at random. It sounded terrible.

Elsa smiled, "That's it, Ettie. You can play."

Mike backed away toward the kitchen. Chandler was inclined to join him. Maybe they needed to discuss a hunting party after all.

Suddenly, the elderly woman sat up tall. She placed both hands on the keyboard with authority and a Bach concerto echoed through the dingy old restaurant as her fingers recalled their skill. Elsa closed her eyes and nodded in time along with the song—one of their father's favorites.

"Now there's something to record," Sydney murmured to Stanley.

"Shush. I'm listening," he replied, but the gruff edge to his voice was gone. Mike and Chandler, almost to the red double doors returned, amazed that Etna was capable of producing such sounds.

Entranced with the dance of ancient fingers, AngelBaby stood closest to the old woman's side, watching every move. Rosie, who had resumed straightening up their area, suddenly sat. Her face relaxed as she allowed the interplay of melodies to return her to a happier time. She took Elvis into her lap. It was a short piece, even by Bach standards, but somehow the room seemed lighter.

"And now a waltz!" cried Elsa.

Etna jumped into the "Waltz of the Flowers" from the *Nutcracker* and Elsa grabbed Chandler by the hands. "Dance with me young man!" Chandler shuffled his feet, but could not match the suddenly nimble Elsa.

"Didn't they teach you this in school?" She gasped between steps.

"Uh no, they did not," he replied and looked around for rescue. Mike was backing toward the kitchen. Suddenly Chandler felt a tap on his shoulder.

"May I cut in?"

He looked down. "Stanley?"

The round-bellied, middle-aged man answered, "Let me show you how it's done, son." Chandler backed away as Stanley bowed to Elsa. "Sydney and I took lessons for two weeks at Arthur Murray just before our boy got married." Elsa curtsied back, and they made their way around the room. Half a head taller than her partner, Elsa smiled as if the fumbling Stanley was Fred Astaire to her Ginger Rogers.

Etna only had a few moments of energy left in her, but it was enough. As she finished the last chord, Elsa and Stanley crashed into a table, and sank into chairs laughing while everyone, even Sydney, applauded. "Bravo! Bravo!"

Etna looked around as if awake for the first time all day and smiled. Then a single tear rolled down her cheek. "Miss Etna, Miss Etna, that was so beautiful. Why are you crying?" asked AngelBaby.

Etna's eyes clouded back over and her sister said, "Maybe I'll tell you later."

She turned to the group. "We used to host a cotillion in our home for young people. Everyone needs to know how to waltz." Etna began to play again, and Elsa stopped her. "No, no darling, you must rest a bit. I will count it out."

In a loud teacher-like voice Elsa commanded, "Everyone turn and face me." Chandler, Mike, Sydney, AngelBaby and Stanley obeyed. "Come on Miss Rosie, you too. United we stand." Rosie put Elvis down and joined the group. "Now, just do what I do," the elderly woman called out. "This is a simple box step: One, Two, Three, One, Two, Three, One, Two, Three. Good!" Within moments they were all chanting to-gether and box-stepping around the room. The old pine floor reverberated in three-quarter time. But before long, Elsa was gasping between commands and had to sit down.

"Miss Elsa, you need to rest," said Chandler.

"Yes, you're probably right. This just brings back such good memories. The young people loved coming to our home." Chandler escorted her back to her chair. "We'll try again this evening," she said, smiling at Stanley, "with partners."

Rosie looked at Mike and he disappeared into the kitchen. After settling the sisters, Chandler joined him. Stanley appeared shortly carrying a gray plastic case.

"Here's the dancing man," said Mike.

Stanley paid no attention to his mocking tone. "Yeah, the folks at Arthur Murray said I was a natural," he boasted, heft-ing his weight from one foot to another. "Those old sisters are something. And that little girl? Oh my."

Mike and Chandler exchanged glances. Was this the same Stanley?

The older man continued. "Look. No one knows any of us are here. This weather could last a week. What if the gas goes out too? This is a real emergency and we've got to do something."

Mike nodded. "I've been trying to pick that old radio apart. No luck yet."

"That's beyond me," said Chandler.

"I could go for help," said Mike. "There's some old snow-shoes up on the wall."

"Don't be ridiculous," said Stanley. "It's at least three miles to anything. Everything's covered up. I hate to admit Sydney's right, but no one is out to rescue anybody in all this."

"Mike was talking about going hunting," offered Chandler.

Stanley held up the plastic case. "No need. If we go easy, the rations will last us three, maybe four days."

"More algae?" asked Chandler.

Stanley nodded, "Yep, but there are a couple of other options in there too. See what you can come up with, Cookie. Miss Elsa was right. United we stand."

The three men shook hands.

# Chapter 12

True to Stanley's promise, Chandler found a wider range of options in the rations. Doing some quick math and mixing and matching, he planned out a menu for the next three days. It was light, but it would do. *At least it's easy, just add water.*

Tonight they would dine on rehydrated mashed potatoes and vegetable stew. A highlight: one freeze-dried pack of cranberries. *Holiday touch.* Sherr was ever close in Chandler's mind. She loved cranberries. He was trying not to think about her tragic Christmas Eve. *Noche Buena* with her family should have been the happiest night of the year. In Puerto Rico's hot climate her mother's body would have to be cared for immediately. Was Sherr preparing it for burial even at this very moment? "Dear God help her," he breathed. *OK Chandler, get it together. You've got guests.*

After serving the food, Chandler raised his water glass. "I'd like to thank the founders of the feast!" Sydney smiled and Stanley looked down at his bowl. "Stanley and Sydney, thank you for sharing your high-octane rations. It'll keep us going. Only one problem, I couldn't find any Twinkies. Sorry, no dessert." His laugh was a bit forced, but Mike played along.

"Well at least they didn't share any powdered fruitcake," he said.

"Ah fruitcake," said Elsa. "We made a famous one every

year." Mike made a face. "When Papa was away during the war, we sent him one at Christmas. Remember, Ettie?" Her sister remained silent. "Apparently it couldn't be delivered so they shipped it back to us. We just left it wrapped up in the tin, and he ate it when he came home the next year." Mike pretended to drop his spoon on the floor and bent down to pick it up, gagging at the thought of fruitcake of any age. "Those cakes were soaked in amaretto. Papa always said it was the best one he'd ever eaten."

"Oh my, that sounds amazing," said Sydney.

"My mother learned the recipe from his mother," continued Elsa, "But I think she made some adjustments. That's where the amaretto came in. She was from Italy."

"You are Italian?" asked Rosie.

"Half. The story is Papa met our mother during the first world war. Somehow he managed to get her back here, or I should say to Knoxville, his hometown in Tennessee." Etna sat in silence, eyes closed. The one headlamp reflecting off the ceiling made Elsa's silver hair and pale skin glow. She wove pictures in the air with her hands as she spoke. AngelBaby thought she looked like an elderly ghost. "After fruitcake," said Elsa, "we would sit around and tell stories until midnight."

Chandler spoke up, "Please do. We need some good stories." The others nodded. Mike fiddled with radio pieces. AngelBaby held Elvis close. Stanley drummed his fingers on the tabletop until Sydney placed her hand on his.

The elderly woman looked around at the group. "I wish I could help you understand how things were when Ettie and I were growing up. It was an enchanted and glamorous time, especially compared to life nowadays—even with the Depression and the wars. But I'll just tell you about our mother and father. He went away to World War I where he served as a medic, and met a beautiful Italian woman, our mother. Ettie is named for Mount Etna. And our younger sister... well anyway, after the war, our parents fixed up the old family farmhouse where he had grown up. Mother had beautiful long black hair." Elsa smiled at AngelBaby and Rosie stroked the girl's hair. "How I loved to comb it when I was a child. Sometimes she would let me after she washed it. It was so heavy in my hands, and smelled of lilacs."

The travelers forgot about the wind and weather for a few moments as they found themselves transported to an earlier time. Elsa continued.

"One day, when Ettie and I came home from school, we found a new baby at the house. It was Erma, our little sister. But soon after her birth, Mama went away. At least that's what Papa said. We asked and asked, we missed her so much. He did too. And as we grew older, we realized she had died and he could not bear to tell us." Elsa broke stride for a moment. "I hope you will never do that to your children. I think he wanted to believe it was all a bad dream and he would wake up one day and she'd be back."

Chandler nodded. Sherr was probably feeling that way right now.

Elsa looked down. "My father was never the same. Our little sister Erma grew up with that same beautiful long black hair. Pictures of her as a young woman look so much like our mother. She couldn't help it, she was Papa's favorite, and because we saw how happy she made him, she was our favorite too. We were happy, even though we missed our mother, and even though times got hard during the Depression. A woman from town, dear Mrs. Owens came every day to help us cook and clean. Ettie and I looked after our little sister. She loved to pump the organ pedals when Ettie played. We all did everything together. Money was tight, but we had what we needed. One of us would wear the pink sweater one day then trade with each other for another day, especially as Erma grew up. And of course, the boys came calling. She was so pretty. And so innocent."

"I still don't understand why, but maybe I do. When the Second World War broke out, Papa volunteered right away. I was put in charge to care for my sisters. Papa looked so handsome in his uniform. I am sure he wanted to return to Italy, the land of his lost love, but he was stationed in Great Britain. That's where we sent the fruitcake. And we wrote him letters every week. But I could not tell him everything. Erma had a sweetheart, a young man we all loved. He was enlisted and sent to the war in the Pacific." Elsa stopped and looked at Rosie and AngelBaby.

Rosie said, "My grandparents used to talk about what a terrible time that was, fighting for independence from the Americans, then the Japanese, then the Americans again."

"I'll never understand it all," Elsa replied. "War is terrible. But that's enough. Rosie, tell us about your family."

"No, no," protested the Filipina. What happened to your younger sister and her sweetheart?"

"He never came back," Elsa resumed. "She was so certain he would. She told me they had been secretly married before he left. A few months later, my little sister Erma, our Papa's angel child, was clearly with child. It was such a scandal. Not like nowadays. Now that I am old, I think Papa might have accepted his grandchild, but we did not think so at the time. And Erma was my responsibility. I failed. Of course, there were a lot of war brides. But Erma was ... Princess Erma. Ettie and I kept her home from school. She was only sixteen. We asked dear Mrs. Owens to help, and she did. She offered her cousin's home a whole state away and I sent Ettie to stay with Erma through the childbirth. Naturally, Erma wanted to keep her child, a little black-haired boy. She named him Robert for his father."

"Again, God bless Mrs. Owens. She offered to care for the boy and Erma could visit as often as she liked. We were so grateful. We paid her everything we could and sent her vegetables from our garden, and fresh milk and eggs. Two years later Papa returned from the war. He was so tired. At first, he took no notice of the housekeeper's new adopted 'nephew' as she called him. But that child had the same look in his eye, the same raven black hair as Erma and our mother. When he came to visit, almost every day, he and Erma were inseparable. A few weeks after returning home, Papa called me into his tiny office. I will never forget that day."

'Tell me the truth,' he said. 'Whose child is that?' He pointed out the window to the shady spot under the apple tree where Erma and Robert (we called him 'Bertie') were at play, laughing together. I looked straight my father and lied. 'Mrs. Owens' younger sister died of the flu last year and little Bertie was sent to her house. She's been bringing him over in the afternoons. Erma's gotten quite attached. Isn't he a dear?'

Papa got a faraway look in his eye. 'Yes. I suppose so.' Nothing was said after that. Bertie became a household fixture. Papa's business took off. Electrical appliances were all the rage after the war and he made a good living in the sales and repair business until he passed away a few years later. Erma waited and waited for her husband to come home. He never did."

"That is so sad," Rosie said, shaking her head.

Elsa nodded. "Yes. It was. She was so certain her husband was locked up in some dreadful prisoner of war camp and would return someday—wasn't she, Ettie?" Etna nodded slowly. "Eventually dear Mrs. Owens died and it seemed time to make things right. I asked Erma about it one night. 'Don't you want to set things straight with Bertie and let him know?' By this time he was a strapping young man, star football player and oh so handsome." Elsa looked at Mike. "Michael, you remind me of him just a bit. Of course he is much older than you now." Mike ran his hand through his bushy hair, smiled a little through his mustache and returned to the radio fragments.

"Erma surprised me. She was not one to ever raise her voice, but she cried out, 'and change everything he knows? And tell him that all this time we were really his family but would never claim him? Oh how could we? How could you? Why now? Why not when Papa was away, or when he first came back from the war?'"

Everyone around the table sat in silence, eyes fixed on Elsa, even Etna paid attention.

"I was stunned. My Princess Erma had hidden her feelings all through the years, wishing for a reality I had denied her. Was Papa so proud, or was I? Just a few weeks later she left home. We didn't see her much over the years."

Etna wheezed a sigh and a tear rolled down her face.

"Her ashes are in an urn in the car," Elsa continued. "We're on our way to spread them on the Shenandoah River."

The room was very quiet for a long time. Then Rosie asked, "What about you Miss Erma and Miss Etna, did you ever get married?"

"Oh there were plenty of beaus and plenty of offers," said Elsa, "But it was wartime. The young men went away, and the few who returned were often maimed—in heart, head or body." She turned to her sister. "But we did have some good times, didn't we Ettie? Like I said, our place became kind of a finishing school for the young people in the area."

"What about Erma's son?" Mike asked.

"Well, Bertie is our only heir. But it was hard, and I realized what a terrible thing I had done, not only to Erma, but to him. After Erma went away, we didn't see him for a long time either. Years. But when he got married and had his own children, I guess he finally forgave me. He usually stops by at Christmas and brings us a ham. This year he'll find the place abandoned. There's a note on the door addressed to him. Instructions from our attorney—it will make quite a Christmas gift, that old place."

"You're not going back?" Stanley said.

"No."

Stanley continued, "But why not?"

Sydney kicked him under the table. "It's none of our business, Stanley."

Elsa clapped her hands. "That's our story, who is next?"

## Chapter 13

Mike rolled the old radio antenna around in his fingers. "So, your Bertie. Is he a motorcycle guy like me?"

"More of an automobile aficionado. He's going to love that Tesla," replied Elsa.

"Maybe sooner than later," Stanley mumbled. Sydney nudged him with her toe.

"Tell us a story, Michael," said Elsa. "Michael is an angel's name."

Mike shook his head. "No angels here—my granddad was Mike, my dad was Mike, and I am just plain old Mike."

Rosie said, "Why are you riding a motorcycle in this snow? Many people ride motorcycles in the Philippines, but it is always hot there."

Mike said, "I know. It's kinda crazy. Originally I was going to stay to the south and work my way back to New Orleans from LA. Then I decided swing up and surprise my mom for Christmas. She hasn't seen me in a while. Didn't look at the weather, just took a left turn onto Highway 81, and a few hours later—well you saw what happened out there. Thanks for turning that light on, man," He nodded at Chandler.

"I didn't know it was on."

"Yeah well, except for my mom, nobody would care if I

got lost. And she hasn't seen me in so long ..." the big man trailed off.

"What happened to you?" asked Rosie.

"Been traveling across the country."

"Yes, but why?"

Mike sighed. "We're all probably gonna die here anyway. So why not? OK. I know I look rough and everything—but I had a repair shop out west that was doing pretty well."

"Motorcycles?" asked Sydney.

"Yeah—mostly, and some cars. Fixed 'em, sold 'em, nothing fancy, but we did good business. People liked that we were independent from any dealership. Good solid work, good reputation. My wife ..." he looked down at his hands. "My wife hated that I used to come home every night with grease on my hands. I was never good enough, even though we made a decent living, and I took real good care of her." He nodded at Elsa. "You're right, I did play football. She was cheerleader captain."

Mike grew silent. All they could hear was the wind moaning around the corners of the old wooden building. He sighed. "I came home from work one day, and there was a car in the driveway. It belonged to a guy I had hired a few months back. Handsome, clean-cut kid—talkative, friendly." Mike placed the antenna on the pile of radio parts with care and looked around at the group. "I won't tell you the rest. Let's just say I went back to the dealership, picked out my favorite bike and left. Been ridin' ever since." He looked at Chandler. "Your wife pretty?"

Chandler said, "She's the most beautiful woman in the world to me."

"Yeah, that's what I thought about my wife too. I was blind-sided."

Chandler shook his head. "Not a good time, man."

"I am sorry for you, Mike," interjected Rosie.

"Yeah, everybody's sorry for Mike now. Don't be. She got what she deserved. Anyway, I'm on my way to see my mom. IF we ever get out of here."

Sydney couldn't help herself. "What did you do?"

Mike gave her an angry look. "None of your business. What would you do?"

"No, I mean, how long have you been on the road?  How do you support yourself?"

"I just stop and work when I need to." He held up his hands. "Greasy hands. I can always find a job. Then I move on." Mike shoved his chair back. "That's it, I don't want to talk about it anymore."

The travelers sat in silence for a moment. The wind suddenly grew louder as if some vicious vortex had settled over the top of the old building. A loud crashing startled them.

"What's that?" cried out AngelBaby.

"Sounds like a tree blew over, maybe several." Mike exclaimed. "Better hope they missed the parking lot."

Everyone except the elderly sisters jumped up and headed for the windows. A couple of cracks in the boards allowed for limited vision, but not everyone could see out at once. There was a little pushing, but Mike gained a spot first. He smashed his face up against the glass, craning his head around to get a view.

"Too dark—can't tell," he said.

"Here let me see," demanded Stanley. The larger man gave way. Stanley bellied up to the window, stretching up to see through the crack in the board. If the situation had been less serious, the others might have laughed at his efforts.

"He's right. No way to tell. We'd have to get the front door open ..."

"Oh dear," Elsa called out from the table. "That sounds dreadfully cold."

Chandler took her cue. "It's not like we could do anything anyway. Let's wait a bit."

Stanley remained fixated on the door, both hands on the heavy-duty door latch. "If we all pushed, we could shove the snow out of the way and get this open."

Chandler pulled Sydney aside. "Can you please get him off that door idea? He gestured back toward the sisters. "We don't need to risk the cold, or not being able to get it back shut."

Sydney nodded, "You're right." She went to her husband's side and whispered something. He reluctantly moved away from the door and the two returned to the table. After trying to peek outside through the crack in the board, Rosie and AngelBaby followed. They could see nothing.

Chandler remained a moment, considering possible scenarios. He prayed for their safety, and for Sherr, then rejoined the group.

Sydney was talking. "We were headed up to the casinos at Atlantic City, *and* we looked at the weather," she said.

"But SOMEONE got us off to a late start," interrupted Stanley. "And we would have made it just fine if you hadn't ..."

Sensing contention, Chandler interrupted. "Hey guys, I really do want to hear your story. But there's something I need to clear up first. Mike, you said something a while ago that's bothering me."

"Knock yourself out man," the motorcyclist said. He had retired to a chair beside the empty fireplace.

"I need to tell you about my wife."

## Chapter 14

"She is the most beautiful woman in the world to me, though she's not a Miss Universe type," Chandler nodded at Rosie. "But she's got this hair. He held his hands up over his head. "It's big and curly like a lion's mane. And she's got this smile that lights up everything around her."

"How did you meet her?" asked AngelBaby.

"That's kind of embarrassing. The short answer is she slammed me in the face with a volleyball."

"And you married her?" the girl continued.

"Yeah I did," he grinned. "I guess there's a little more to the story. Sherr's dad was a lightweight boxing champ back in the day."

Rose interjected, "We have some very famous boxers in the Philippines."

"He may have fought some of them," Chandler nodded. "But along the way, he decided to stop boxing and start working with street kids in San Juan doing sports programs and stuff. He and his wife run a home for kids. Anyway, I guess Sherr inherited those boxing reflexes. She is super athletic. Her high school team was invited to play a tournament in Florida and she got recruited for a full ride at the University of Florida.

"That's a big deal," said Sydney.

"Yeah. She says there was hardly time to study, but it sure

saved her family a lot of money. When she graduated, she moved to Richmond for a high school coaching job. I had just moved up there. I met her at a church picnic. She forgot the game was just for fun and slammed me right in the nose with a volleyball —bam!" Chandler smacked the table. "My nose swelled up so much I could barely see. We ended up at the emergency room, and I never let her forget it." Everybody laughed. He shook his head. Then his laugh halfway ended in a sob.

"But Mike, this woman is the kind of girl who gets the news —at Christmas, our first married Christmas—that her family needs her. And she goes. It was the right thing for her to do. And I should have gone with her." Chandler put his head in his hands. "Stupid me. The Angelino brothers offered a bonus if I'd come check this place out. She's been paying most of the bills while I finished school. I felt terrible for her mom, but I figured she could go see her folks and I could earn some extra cash."

"And put a light on in the storm," said Elsa.

"I did not turn on that light," Chandler replied.

"Somebody did," said Mike.

Chandler ignored him. "Sherr's folks have this old farm close to the city. Lots of space for kids and lots of chores to keep everybody busy. And, Sherr's mom? She is one firecracker." He paused, "I guess I should say she was."

Elsa took Etna's hand. The group sat quietly for a moment. Chandler continued, trying to control the tremble in his voice. "I imagine she and Sherr's dad had some knock-down drag-outs before everybody mellowed out. That was one straight up all-or-nothing woman. She ran an accounting business. Sherr takes more after her dad. They never had any other kids."

"Maybe there were health problems early on," said Sydney.

"Yeah maybe, but now I cannot imagine what Sherr is going through right now. She's getting ready for a funeral. At Christmas." He fell silent again, distraught.

"She is with her father when he needs her more than any-body," said Elsa. "It's so hard to lose someone you love."

"And I wasn't with her when she needed ME." Chandler stood up and paced around the room looking at the pictures on the walls. "Who were *these* people? What were they up against? Like this lady. She looks happy in the picture, but what was really going on in her life?" he grabbed a framed black and white newspaper clipping off the wall and almost threw it on the table. A young woman with a shiny, black beehive hairdo smiled from the back of a convertible in a parade. The headline read, "Paw Paw Queen, 1962: Betty Evans."

"What is a Paw Paw?" asked AngelBaby.

Stanley surprised them all by answering, "It's a fruit native to North America. Some people compare it to a mango."

Sydney interrupted, "No, it's nothing like a mango."

Rosie agreed. "There is nothing like a mango."

Stanley continued," I guess they grow around here. We had 'em in West Virginia, but only out in the country."

"I thought all West Virginia was out in the country," said Mike.

"You should see that country," said Stanley.

"Oh I've seen it."

Sydney broke in. "Nineteen sixty-two. That's the year Stan-ley and I were both born. I have pictures of my mother with that hairdo. "No hairspray for me," she rubbed her eyes. "My mom and dad always went to a big fancy Christmas party every year with their Navy friends. That was a sight." She looked at Stanley, "No Christmas parties for us, not in a long time. The boys are busy with their own kids out west."

"Your boys?" said Rosie.

"Yes, we have twin sons. They both got into technology pretty young. Chips off the old blocks I guess. Ha. Chips." She looked at Stanley," "Not like us. We had to learn everything from scratch. Stanley and I went to MIT—that's where we met. I was a TA and he was in my class."

Elsa looked puzzled. "What is a Tee A?"

"Teaching Assistant. I was there on scholarship and part of the deal was grading and tutoring."

"I was her star student," said Stanley.

"You became a star *after* I explained some things," Sydney retorted.

Chandler returned to the table. "And the Bentley?"

Mike looked up, "Bentley?"

Chandler nodded. "Right out there in the snow."

Mike glanced at the window even though it was completely dark outside.

Stanley said, "Yeah, if it's not smashed under a tree." He glanced at the front door and felt the nudge of Sydney's toe. "We learned a few things along the way about data."

Sydney popped in, "Data works the way data works, whether its radio signals, business trends or cards."

"You won a Bentley in a poker game?" asked Mike.

"Well ..." the two looked at each other. "Sort of," said Stanley. "Let's just say our stock portfolios have done really well. We did some mapping, made some educated guesses, worked out an algorithm or two, out-did a 'randomizer' ..."

"Shut UP, Stanley."

And they still let you in up at Atlantic City?" Mike said.

"Oh we make sure we lose too," Sydney glanced over her shoulder as if someone was listening. "Just enough."

Mike shook his head. "I'm glad we're not playin' cards tonight—you'd wipe us all out."

"Maybe. Good luck? Bad luck? Probability. What are the odds and how do you read 'em?" Stanley paused and looked at his wife for confirmation. "But this is our last trip."

Sydney nodded, "We've raised the boys, we're done. You might say this is just a sentimental journey. Our divorce lawyer is lined up for mid-January."

Stanley agreed. "No hard feelings."

Sydney crossed her arms. "Of course not. Got to go while you're still young enough to live a little."

"And have the funds to play with," Stanley added. They both sounded completely matter-of-fact as if parting ways in middle age had always been the long-term plan. Nobody knew what to say. It was a relief when Rosie spoke up.

"Are you going to teach us to waltz some more tonight, Miss Elsa? With partners this time?"

Elsa shook herself away from staring at Stanley and Sydney. "I'm trying to make sense out of all this. Yes, yes Rosie, we must dance. It is time. Ettie, can you play for us?" Etna, who had mostly been staring at the wall for the last thirty minutes smiled at her sister and slowly made her way back to the pump organ.

Stanley pulled Sydney aside, "Stay away from that guy Mike. He practically admitted to bumping off his wife, and probably her boyfriend too."

"Shut up, Stanley."

"And did you see how he perked up over the Bentley? I'm telling you, watch out."

"You're the one that brought up the randomizer," answered his wife. "And you really think I'd run off with him after we split up?"

"If we ever make it out of here? Yes."

Sydney rolled her eyes. "I'm not his type. And besides, why should you care?"

Taking command once again, Elsa directed them. "The box step you learned this morning is the same. Now the gentleman leads and his lady follows. Sydney and Stanley, over here. Mike and Rosie, over there. Chandler, please help the baby Angel."

Stanley and Sydney squared off like boxers casting tall, sharp shadows in the headlamp lighting. Rosie was impossibly short for Mike and AngelBaby even more so for Chandler. Rosie smiled up at Mike. He glowered back at her and glanced over at Chandler and AngelBaby, very much at arm's length from one another. Elsa made the rounds correcting posture and setting frame. "Now Ettie!" After a couple of false starts, Etna found her way into the "Skater's Waltz." The wind seemed to pick up the tune and AngelBaby imagined skaters blown around on the ice by a gale.

Chandler took a couple of faltering steps, then looked down at her. "I'm sorry—I just can't dance tonight."

She shook his hand. "It's OK. We don't have to. I dance all the time."

They returned to their chairs and watched Rosie try to keep her feet out from under Mike's clumsy boots. Finally he said,

"Look, I'm sorry ma'am, I am just not a dancer." He jammed his hands in his pockets and excused himself.

Elsa took Rosie in hand and the two continued across the scarred pine floor for a moment—then stopped to watch Stanley and Sydney who were moving in time and together with ease, if not grace.

"Data in motion," said Sydney. She and Stanley grinned at each other for the first time in two days.

## Chapter 15

"Miss Elsa, the waltz reminds me of one of our traditional dances from the Philippines," said Rosie rubbing her offended foot. "I will show you. But first I need to find some long poles." She cast around the room and finally spied two long cane fishing poles hung over one of the windows. "Mike," she said, "Could you please bring those down for us?" she pointed with her lips at the poles.

"What do you want?" he asked.

AngelBaby answered, "she means those two long poles up there over the window."

"Oh. I don't get the lip thing."

"We point that way, with our lips." AngelBaby demonstrated a pert pout.

"OK. Whatever."

It took Mike a few moments and more muttering to pry the cane poles loose. As he pulled them down, Rosie caught them and wiped them free of trailing cobwebs. "That is good, thank you. Now we need two short pieces of wood." She said something in dialect to AngelBaby who began stalking the perimeter of the dining room, scouring the walls and shelves.

"What about this one, Auntie Rosie?" she held up an old hammer.

"That's a little short, but maybe it will work. We need another one, or something like it."

"Here you go," said Mike, bringing an old hatchet he found propped up by the fireplace.

The others watched with curiosity as Rosie laid first the hammer, then the hatchet on the floor about eight feet apart. She placed the two cane poles in parallel across the top. It looked like a ladder with most of its middle steps missing.

Rosie then grabbed Chandler by the hand and asked him to kneel on the floor behind the hammer. She placed the cane poles in his hands. Directly across from him, AngelBaby knelt behind the hatchet. She took up the opposite ends, one pole in each hand. Rosie began clapping her hands. "One, Two, Three, One, Two, Three ..." AngelBaby guided Chandler to thump the poles downward twice then raise them up in the air on "Three" and clack them together. He quickly caught on.

Once they got the rhythm going, Rosie took off her shoes and socks revealing an elegant purple pedicure. She stood next to the clacking poles. As they parted, she dipped one foot in the middle. Just before they closed together, she lightly skipped through to the other side. She repeated the motion and skipped back. Her feet found openings at just the right time.

"Be careful dear!" said Elsa.

Rosie smiled. "No worries." She began an intricate pattern of stepping through the clacking canes, never once losing her balance or a toe. Pudgy at best, as she swayed her arms and body, Rosie was transformed into a picture of grace. "Faster!" she demanded.

Chandler and AngelBaby complied and nearly doubled

their speed. She responded with energy channeled through taut posture and precise footwork.

AngelBaby began singing a lilting tune that bounced off the drumming poles. The floor vibrated like a big bass drum that drowned out the wind. Rosie moved faster than anyone would have thought possible through the flashing, clashing beat, until with a final flamenco-like flourish, she completed the dance. Everyone applauded. Chandler wiped his sleeve across his forehead. It came back wet.

"Bravo! Bravo!" said Stanley

Even Mike was impressed.

"OK, now your turn," Rosie said.

Mike shook his head in refusal. "You go Chan man—let's see what you got."

Chandler wished Sherr was here. She would catch on quickly.

Elsa saw his face, "Don't worry young man. This is a time to dance."

Rosie took Chandler's place on the floor behind the hammer.

Mike made a face and held his nose when Chandler took off his boots and socks. But the younger man ignored him. He was surprised how soothing the bare wooden floor felt to his bare feet. *Like Grandma Nonnie's house.*

"Just step across," said Rosie.

She and AngelBaby moved the cane poles slowly.

"Ouch!" The first couple of attempts caught first one foot then the other. "I'm too clumsy." Chandler turned to sit down.

"No, no, you are OK. You just need a little help. Angel-Baby!" Rosie motioned toward Chandler with her lips.

AngelBaby looked up at Mike. "Would you take the poles please, Mr. Mike?" Mike grunted, but did his best, complaining under his breath all the way. Rosie gave him a quick tutorial and the clacking soon resumed.

AngelBaby joined Chandler beside the poles. She held out her hands. "Follow me."

"Very slowly," Rosie said to Mike. Thump, thump, whack! Thump, thump, whack!

AngelBaby showed Chandler how to step through the clacking trap, and back again. Once he realized how the rhythm worked, he lost his fear and realized the "whack" would not catch him. "It's like double-dutch jump rope," he said. "Sherr taught me." The girl hopped out and Chandler kept going for a few moments, forgetting his sorrow for the moment in the drone of the poles.

"Well done!" Elsa and the rest applauded as Rosie and Mike laid the poles to rest.

"Chandler, you're a natural," said Sydney. She whispered to Stanley, "It's a good thing we could waltz. I don't know about this one and I am NOT taking my shoes off."

"We could always teach them the chicken dance," he replied.

"Shut up, Stanley."

## Chapter 16

"Rosie, what's your story?" asked Chandler, trying to keep his mind off events in Puerto Rico.

AngelBaby picked Elvis up and looked at her aunt. She had heard rumors.

Rosie looked at her niece and sighed, then turned to the rest of the group. "I was one of the best dancers at my school. Until Angel's mother, my little sister, started to grow up." She nodded at AngelBaby. "Well, actually she was my half-sister. Our father kept two families. Everyone knew about it. But anyway, my mother always told me to study hard so I could become a nurse because those were good-paying jobs. You could also work abroad and earn more money."

"My father favored his other family over us. I always wanted to show him my good grades so he would be proud of me. He saw my hard work and when it was time to go to nursing school, he supported me the first year. The second year he gave me less money because the other family had more children and school fees. Then he died."

"I had one year left in my program. I decided I needed to go to a bigger city so I could work and save money for school. I wrote a letter to one of my mother's relatives in Manila and asked if I could stay with them. They had young children.

Maybe I could take care of them in exchange for room and board."

"My mother was very angry with me when she learned my plan. 'It is very dangerous, there are many bad people there,' she said. 'You can just stay and work here.' But I wouldn't listen. I was ready for a new place. Manila seemed like it would be a much more exciting place than our town. My brother said, 'Once you get a job and a place, I will come join you.' He was ready for something else too. My oldest brother was already married by then and I knew he could watch after our mother."

She looked at AngelBaby. "You have not heard this part of the story, darling, but now you are old enough." AngelBaby looked up from petting Elvis. What version would Aunt Rosie share?

"Like I said, I was one of the best dancers in my school. There was a tourist area in Manila that catered to foreign guests. I heard they were hiring and paid well, so I went there to see. Every night so many tour buses and taxis arrived. Japanese, Koreans, Australians, Europeans, Americans—ready for entertainment. The evening started out with the traditional dances, like the *Tinikling*, the one I just showed you. And then dancing with candles in our hands and on top of our heads." She lifted her hands up and grazed the short hair on top of her head.

"That sounds risky," said Sydney.

"Yes, we had to practice a lot. Once the candles were lit, you could really get burned. I had a friend ..."

Elvis suddenly began to bark. Rosie looked at AngelBaby who was staring at her in fascination. She continued.

"My partner was a handsome young man from Mindanao. He was always so kind. He helped me learn the traditional

Muslim dances. I know I am quite fat now, but I was a pretty girl then and we wore beautiful costumes. The other girls were jealous because he was very kind to me."

"One night after our usual performance, one of the girls came to me and said, 'You can make a lot more money by working late hours at private parties for the tourists. They give very good tips.' I was very interested. School fees were high and I needed to move away from my relative's house soon. They did not treat me like a family member. More like a servant. But I did not have enough money for my own place yet."

"When I mentioned the late parties to my partner, he said, 'No. When it gets late they get drunk and dangerous.' I laughed, 'If they're drunk, they can't hurt me.' But I listened to him and did not go. At the house where I was staying things began to get worse. The older son returned from working abroad and he began to follow me with his eyes. The night he came to my room ..." she looked at AngelBaby who had stopped petting Elvis and was hanging on to every word. "I fought him off. The next morning I packed my bag and left. That night I went to my first late party. They tipped well."

AngelBaby turned her eyes back to the dog. Rosie continued. "There was a Japanese businessman who brought new guests every few weeks. He liked me and began to tell me I should go to Tokyo where I could really earn a lot of money. I could work as a maid in someone's house by day, and if that was not enough, earn extra money weekends dancing in the clubs. Again, my friend said, I should not go. He still cared for me even though I was working the late parties."

"I wrote to my brother and told him I was going to Tokyo. He was so upset he made a long-distance phone call. He said,

'The Japanese are cruel. They will not treat you well. Don't forget what they did here during the war.' I said, 'The war was a long time ago. I am just dancing. I need the money for school.' So I went. The businessman paid for my plane ticket. I am not going to share all the details with you. I stayed in Tokyo for many years and I became very popular. I learned to speak Japanese. I learned to ride subways. I learned that some Japanese people are cruel, but I also came to admire some of them. I survived, though I never went back to nursing school."

"After many years Typhoon Yolanda hit my hometown, Tacloban. The news reported thousands of deaths. I had to return to check on my family, no matter what they thought of me. I had money, I could help. I found our city devastated. My mother was gone. And my half-sister, my rival in school and for my father's affections was gone. But she had this tiny, beautiful angel baby."

Rosie looked across the room at her niece. She remained engrossed with Elvis and did not look up. "I became very involved helping rebuild the community. When people are desperate, they don't care so much about your reputation. I guess everyone who was scandalized was either dead or gone. Even the priest said thank you. And this AngelBaby grew up and made a TikTok video. When we got the e-mail about coming to New York, there was no question that I would be the one to bring her. Manila? Tokyo? New York? All big cities are the same."

Rosie grew silent. She looked at AngelBaby who looked away. She said something in the dialect and the girl returned an answer and a small smile, then hugged Elvis close.

"What about your young man?" Asked Elsa, "The one who told you not to go to the late party?"

"I don't know what happened to him, "said Rosie. But I wish him the best. He was always only kind to me, like a sweet brother."

The conversation was interrupted by a blaring alarm and announcement from someone's cellphone. "The National Weather Service recommends that everyone seek shelter or remain where you are. This storm is expected to last for another 24 hours. Record snowfalls and high winds expected. Shelter in place and stay off the roads."

"Hey, whose phone is that?" yelled Chandler.

"Mine" said Stanley.

"Can I please send a message to Sherr?"

Stanley looked at Sydney. "It's down to the last bar."

"Give him the phone Stanley," she said.

Stanley reached into his back pocket and pulled out his cellphone. Chandler grabbed it and typed in Sherr's number.

**Hi sweetheart it's me Chandler on Stanley's phone I'm so sorry about your mom!**

He muttered, "C'mon. Send—send!"

The little Delivered confirmation showed up.

A text returned.

**Who is this?**

"Auggghhh!" Chandler furiously engaged fingers and thumbs to reply.

**This is your husband Chandler—stuck in a snowstorm. Battery out, borrowing a friend's phone. So sorry about your mom! I miss u, I can't believe she passed away!!! So sorry!!!**

He stood staring at the device in his hands – the battery was down to its last bar and fading fast.

**Mom?**

Chandler texted back:

**U said she was gone. I'm so sorry**

**Mom's not dead. She went to the...** and the phone blanked out.

Chandler stood shaking, eyes glued to the screen. "She's not dead!!!!" he yelled. "Sherr's mom went somewhere, I don't know where, but she is NOT dead!!!" Everyone began clapping and shaking hands. Elvis ran around in circles wagging his tail.

"Praises be!" said Elsa. "Have some brandy!" She handed the flask to Chandler, who took a sip and choked and passed it around. Everyone laughed and choked and laughed some more. Even Etna smiled.

## Chapter 17

"This is a *Noche Buena*! A VERY good night!" said Chandler. One little phone message made it all the way north from Puerto Rico to Stanley's phone and changed everything. "Now I could dance and mean it," he laughed. "But, let's cook instead." As he headed to the kitchen he called over his shoulder, "See what y'all can do to make this place festive!"

Elsa told Mike to find something "Christmassy" they could use for a centerpiece while she began digging around in the crocodile valises.

Mike turned to Sydney for help. She laughed. "I usually ask other people to do this stuff, but let's see what we can find." Stanley came along with them and actually made the first selection—a set of pewter candlesticks half-hidden behind some knickknacks. AngelBaby found a porcelain angel. Rosie discovered a stash of pinecones, and it became a game after that. When they returned to the sisters, they found a white satin sheet stretched across the tables. It smelled of lavender. Elsa praised their efforts, delighting over each find as if it was a treasure. She sent AngelBaby to the closet beside the Ladies room to bring back candles.

In the kitchen, Chandler rummaged through Stanley and Sydney's ration stash. Most of the packets were single-serving size. *The fancier the restaurant the smaller the portions,* he tried to console himself. It ended up being a bit of this and that. But when he pushed back into the dining room, he was amazed at the view. The headlamp was shut off. Candlelight glowed across a gorgeous Christmas table.

"Festive!" he said. "I should have put you all to work a long time ago!"

Everyone was ready to eat. The meal did not take long and Chandler was pretty sure they were all still a little hungry when the food was gone, but no one complained.

Afterwards, Mike drew Chandler aside. "Let's light a fire," he said, nodding toward the hearth. "No, not the chairs," he added as Chandler began to protest. "I'll go out back. I bet I can find something to burn."

"It's dark," said Chandler, "and really, really cold."

"Yeah, but I need some air," the big man replied.

"Like when you go to your cousin's house for Christmas and you can't get away?"

Mike nodded. "Yep. And don't tell anyone. They'll just worry."

"OK, but don't be long, or we'll have to send out a search party and you know how that will go."

"Stanley and Sydney probably have some kinda heat sensing infrared binoculars," Mike smirked, "they'd find me." The two returned to the kitchen where Mike pulled on his boots and coat, wrapped a scarf over his ears and jammed his hat over the top of it all.

The blast of cold air from the opening door rushed in smelling of pine. For a brief moment, the wind died and the snow ceased. An early moon, peeping out from behind a cloud, cast a faint glimmer on the drifts. "You're lucky man, this must be the eye of the storm," said Chandler.

Mike nodded and pointed toward the dim outline of a shed a few yards away. "I'm going to check that first."

"You sure you don't want those snowshoes?" Chandler asked.

"Naw—too much trouble and too much attention. I can get from here to there."

Mike took a deep breath and plunged into the snow. He sank up to mid-thigh on the first step and up to his waist on the next. But it was still powdery enough that he was able to half-walk, half-wade through. Chandler watched for a moment, shivering, before heaving the door shut. Was it just last night when he had pulled Rosie and AngelBaby in through this door? And not long after that when he had made his own ranting exit? Time seemed to have stretched. He turned and put some water on the stove. *That guy is gonna need some thawing out when he gets back.* Tentative sounds from the pump organ squawked from the other room. Clearly not Etna.

Chandler turned back to the window. The moon had disappeared behind clouds, but he could see the flashlight bobbing along. Mike was three-quarters of the way to the shed. The pan on the stove began to steam. Chandler turned the heat down. The double doors creaked as Stanley pushed his way into the kitchen. "Where's Mike?"

Chandler nodded toward the window, "Went to get some firewood for the fireplace."

"Son of a gun."

"Yeah—its cold out there."

"Do you think he could take a look around front to see if that tree landed on my car?"

Chandler turned toward the older man. "Really? I hope he makes it to the shed and back." A tortured version of *chopsticks* from the pump organ turned lively.

Stanley winced and shook his head "Well, I would sure not want to go out there."

"Me neither," Chandler agreed. "I hope he can find something to burn."

"It was a stupid idea. We've got heat. We've got light. And even if there is something, that old roof is probably leaky—it'll be all wet." Chandler was tired of Stanley's negativity, but he had to admit he might be right.

The two watched and waited in silence. Just when Chandler began thinking about a search party, the flashlight glow reappeared. Snow-heavy cloud banks rolled back into formation as the wind regained power. The eye of the storm was no longer upon them.

Mike plowed on, stopping every couple of steps to adjust his load. It kept bogging down in the deep snow. By the time he got to the door, the big man was barely crawling. He stumbled in red-faced, soaked and gasping with the cold.

"What the heck did you find?" asked Stanley.

"P-p-pallets. There were a bunch of pallets stacked up in that shed," he said. "Thought I'd never find somethin' to tie 'em together with—then I saw this old rope—probably off a clothesline or something."

"You've got to get out of those wet clothes," commanded Stanley.

Chandler grabbed a blanket and tossed it to Mike who

stripped down. Shivering, he wrapped the blanket around himself and stepped out of the sodden black pile of boots, jeans, socks, sweatshirt and coat. "My hat's still dry," he said, leaving it on.

"Stand by the stove, man. Breathe in some steam. Warm up your lungs." Chandler had no clue if that was a good idea, but it seemed to make sense.

Mike bent over the boiling pot of water and breathed in. Little streams of water slicked down his legs. He raised his head and shook it, flinging droplets off his beard. "That wood may be a bit wet, but I betcha we can get it to start."

"We can always pour brandy on it if we need to," said Stanley, "Though we might have to arm wrestle the old lady for it. Ha!"

"Right," said Chandler. "Mike if you're not too frozen and you don't think you'll scare the ladies too much, let's give it a try."

*****

The pump organ, manned by Sydney and Rosie with AngelBaby on the pedals, stopped abruptly as the three men strode in from the kitchen. Stanley led the way, followed by Mike, strategically clutching his blanket and Chandler bearing a pallet.

"Ladies, we have firewood."

The vision of Mike clothed only in a blanket was enough to command attention, and he realized a little too late the blanket was not as big as he wished. He stood to the side, flanked by Rosie as Stanley and Sydney fussed over starting the fire.

Chandler returned to the kitchen for more pallets. He grabbed the hammer and began prying out nails. The old wood came apart easily. After several attempts they finally coaxed the damp wood to burn by using the candles. No brandy sacrificed. No one cared that it was a little smoky. They realized the pallets would not last long. Mike did not offer to go back out for more.

Determined to make the most of the blaze, the travelers scooted chairs up in a semi-circle around the hearth. Thinking back to youth camp days, Chandler went to the wall and pulled down the dusty guitar. It still had five out of six strings, and when he turned the tuning peg a little to test them, they held. He strummed a couple of chords. Rosie clapped her hands. "You must play."

Chandler smiled, "I'm not very good—anybody else want to try?"

No one offered. He played a D-chord and began to hum softly, "Silent night ... holy night ..." Rosie and AngelBaby joined in, followed by Elsa who was crackly and off-tune. Etna nodded and smiled a little. Sydney hummed as well. Stanley held his hands out to the fire. Mike looked like he was falling asleep, the blanket beginning to sag from his shoulders. Rosie pulled it up around him and he smiled, eyes closed. Elvis lay at his feet. If someone had looked in the window, they might have thought it was a family portrait in the making.

*****

"Now Chandler, you must read us the Christmas story," said Elsa. "It's tradition. From the book of Luke."

"I don't have a bible," said Chandler.

"Check the organ seat," she replied.

Below the frayed needlepoint seat cushion, beside a child's faded primer and an old hymnbook, he found a black, worn, leather-bound volume, the front faintly embossed with "Holy Bible" in fancy script. "How did you know?" Chandler asked Elsa as he returned.

"These old places often held church services back in the day," she offered up. "Traveling preachers and such. Gran Gran may have been a good Baptist or Methodist. You never know."

He turned to the second chapter of Luke. As he read he heard his grandmother Nonnie's voice. Her rhythm of speech became his own:

*In those days a decree went out from Caesar Augustus that all the world should be enrolled. This was the first enrollment, when Quirinius was governor of Syria. And all went to be enrolled, each to his own city. And Joseph also went up from Galilee, from the city of Nazareth, to Judea, to the city of David, which is called Bethlehem, because he was of the house and lineage of David, to be enrolled with Mary, his betrothed, who was with child. And while they were there, the time came for her to be delivered. And she gave birth to her first-born son and wrapped him in swaddling cloths, and laid him in a manger, because there was no place for them in the inn.*

"The inn," Chandler repeated. He looked around at the drowsy Mike; Stanley and Sydney engrossed by the flames; auntie, niece and dog all wrapped up together in a yellow polka-dot blanket; and the elderly sisters. Elsa caught his glance and smiled back at him.

*And in that region there were shepherds out in the field, keeping watch over their flock by night. And an angel of the Lord appeared to them, and the glory of the Lord shone around them, and they were filled with fear. And the angel said to them, "Be not afraid; for behold, I bring you good news of a great joy which will come to all the people; for to you is born this day in the city of David a Savior, who is Christ the Lord.*

*And this will be a sign for you: you will find a babe wrapped in swaddling cloths and lying in a manger." And suddenly there was with the angel a multitude of the heavenly host praising God and saying, "Glory to God in the highest, and on earth peace among men with whom he is pleased!*

*"When the angels went away from them into heaven, the shepherds said to one another, "Let us go over to Bethlehem and see this thing that has happened, which the Lord has made known to us." And they went with haste, and found Mary and Joseph, and the babe lying in a manger. And when they saw it they made known the saying which had been told them concerning this child; and all who heard it wondered at what the shepherds told them. But Mary kept all these things, pondering them in her heart. And the shepherds returned, glorifying and praising God for all they had heard and seen, as it had been told them.*

Chandler closed the yellowed old pages with care and lay the book in his lap. "This reading always makes me think about my grandmother Nonnie." He looked around the group. "You would have liked her." He gazed into the glow of the fire, "She saved my life."

"Tell us about your grandmother, Chandler," said Elsa. "What happened?"

The young man, firelight reflected in his dark eyes, shook

his head. "It's not a pretty story. I remember learning she was way too young when she had my mom. And that it wasn't her choice to get pregnant.   I felt so angry I wanted to go to hell and kill the guy, even though he was already dead. I know. Not very rational, but I was 15." Mike opened his eyes and sat up to listen.

"My mom was still my mom, and she was alive, and I was alive, but why? Because my Nonnie suffered a terrible injustice. I couldn't look at anything the same after that. I stopped trusting everything and everybody I knew. I started trying to figure out the dark side of everything first so I could stay ahead of it. It was a miserable time. Then this new kid was sent to my school to 'get him away from gang influences.'" Chandler fluttered his fingers in air quotes and nearly dropped the bible on the floor. Catching it, he continued.

"He was new, he was cool, and he just took up where he left off. He got me and a bunch of my friends to agree to always look out for each other, no matter what. I told myself it was all just a stupid game. Then he started challenging us. How much could you get away with and not get caught? Petty crime stuff. My mom was working two jobs. My stepdad was on the road a lot. As long as my grades were OK, they didn't notice much." He shrugged his shoulders. "But the ante kept going up. And up."

"The first time they put me in 'juvie,' I was 16. If they thought the kid at my school was a bad influence, they should have seen what went on there. At any rate, as soon as my grandmother found out about it, she took the bus up to Decatur and hauled me back with her to Alabama. I guess that judge realized she meant business. Maybe he figured out God was on her side.

At any rate, he released me to her care. I was so mad. Grandma Nonnie took me away from my school, my friends, my girlfriend—she saved my life." Everyone seemed mesmerized by the flying sparks and hungry flames, and Chandler wasn't sure they cared, but at this point he was telling the story for his own sake.

"We had been in church my whole life—you know the 'clean up the kids and go show yourself to your neighbors version.' At Nonnie's? I think that woman spent more time at church than not. But it was different. She just lived and breathed Jesus. She'd wake up singing and she'd pray over any food so happy you'd think it was a big fat steak. Even at my angriest, I could not fight her. She'd just look at me and grin. 'Now Chandler—you don't let that old devil win. You're a child of the King!' she'd say—and she'd get me to laughing with her." He mimicked a little old lady voice and AngelBaby giggled. He grinned back at her.

"We were sitting in church on Christmas Eve and I was ready for the whole Christmas story—again. The little kids in their bathrobes were set to walk in and meet the baby Jesus. You know the whole deal. Mary is twice Joseph's size and the kid in the angel outfit is slapping everybody else with his wings every time he turns around." A piece of wood on the fire slipped down and sent up a massive shower of sparks. Stanley leaned over and poked at it with a stick.

"Then somebody's nephew from out of town was asked to read the Christmas story. He said, 'I know you're expecting me to read from the book of Luke, but I want to read you my favorite Christmas scripture: from the book of Philippians. Chapter two.' Now even I knew the Christmas story is not in Philippians, there are no shepherds or anything. I leaned over to whisper some smart remark about the new guy to my grandma. When I looked at her, she had that old worn Bible of hers already open to the spot and it was all underlined. As he read she mouthed the words right along with him. 'For being in very nature God, he did not consider equality with God something to be grasped, but made himself *nothing*, taking on the very appearance of a man. And being in very nature man, he humbled himself and became obedient unto death, even death on the cross.'"

"You memorized it," said Elsa. Chandler nodded.

"Then that guy pointed at the little kid angels and shepherds and said, 'This scripture tells what happened before we get to the earth-side of the Christmas story. It's the prequel. Imagine heaven, if you can, then imagine going from that, to inside a human womb. Jesus left heaven for a single-cell existence inside a Jewish teenager. Our Creator, set aside all his power and joined his creation. He developed as a baby and was born. And he didn't stop there. He, God, walked around dusty Judea for his whole thirty-three years and all he did was love, and teach and heal. Then he did what he came here for. He died so he could give us the greatest gift: life with him forever. He knew there was no other way. We couldn't save ourselves, though a whole lot of us try.'

My grandmother Nonnie was nodding along with him, eyes closed and tears running down her face. I don't remember the rest of that night at church. I just kept going back to the thought of God zapping himself into an embryo, and it blew my mind."

Pieces of pallet wood shifted again with a pop. Mike opened his eyes. "You went to juvie?"

"'Fraid so."

Stanley looked at Sydney, "We're in the care of a criminal."

"Shut up, Stanley."

Rosie said, "Let me try the guitar now please." Chandler handed it to her. With practiced hands she tapped a couple of strings, held it up to her ear and adjusted the pegs ever so slightly. Rosie gently plucked above the round mouth of the guitar. Eyes closed, she began to sing and AngelBaby joined in. "O holy night, the stars were brightly shining, it was the night of our dear savior's birth." They began in soft tones. It was hard to tell who was singing harmony. When they raised their voices together at the end they pierced all darkness with perfect clarity. The room itself seemed to expand with the song. Then, cradling the guitar, Rosie ended the carol the way it had begun, slowly plucking each string until the last note fluttered over the fire and rose up the chimney.

No one said anything for a long time. Then murmuring "good night," they went to bed.

## Chapter 18

Chandler woke up early (much too early given how late they had stayed up). He saw a little pink sock sitting on the kitchen table in front of him, lumpy and bulging. "Santa?" As he picked it up, bright green and yellow foil-wrapped candies tumbled out. Nothing he recognized from the candy aisle. He picked one up. "Chocolate-covered mango." A little piece of paper slipped out, hand lettered "*Maligayon Pasko* Chandler!" with "Merry Christmas" in parentheses below and a smiley face. Filipino Santa.

The lumpy match to the little pink sock lay propped up by the side of the snoring Mike. Chandler smiled. It was just the sort of thing Sherr would have done.

He looked around the kitchen. It was mostly clean but bore reminders of the small plates meal. Wishing for coffee, Chandler unwrapped one of the chocolate mango candies. It might help. The chocolate was not too sweet, and the mango wasn't bad. He reached for another piece. "Too early for noise man," Mike mumbled from the countertop.

"It's Christmas and the sun is shining, I bet we're going to get out of here today!"

Mike started to roll over, then woke up enough to catch himself before going over the side of the countertop. The little pink sock hit the floor.

"What's that?" he said, eyes still closed.

"Santa."

"Whatever," the big man mumbled.

Chandler laughed. "Your sweats are over there—thanks for the loan." Glad to be back in his own clothes (mostly dry) Chandler put water on to heat. As it warmed, he picked through what was left of the ration stash. *Hot chocolate? Algae comes in many disguises.* Finding only four packets, he added enough steaming water to stretch across eight cups. Then for fun, he chopped up the candy and added that too. *That'll amp it up a little.*

Hands full of warm cups, Chandler pushed through the red double doors. A faint scent of wood smoke still lingered in the dining room. He smiled at the ladder-back chairs around the fireplace—intact. The room looked empty, though snores emanated from beside the pump organ. He heard women's voices from the hallway to the Ladies restroom.

Chandler placed the steaming cups on the table. Real sunlight was pouring through cracks in the boards nailed up over the lower half of Gran Gran's front windows. Hardly thinking twice, he dashed back through the kitchen and pushed his way out the back door. Scrabbling through the deep powdery snow, he scooped it aside with his bare hands, ignoring the cold. Back to the basement door, down the steps, and in the glow of the octopus, he saw his prize. Grabbing the rusty coal shovel he returned through the kitchen and tried to open the front door. He pushed as hard as he could but could not move it. Laying the shovel beside the door, he ran back to the kitchen, banging the doors as he went. Mike was pulling on his sweats, "Thanks man," he said then held up the little pink sock. "Did you uh, lose somethin? What's this?"

Chandler ignored him. "Hey, I think we can shovel our way out now. Snowplows might be out. I want to make sure they know we're here. Can you help me get the front door open?" The big man joined him beside the front door. "How deep do you think that snow is?" Chandler asked.

"It's probably drifted all over the porch. No tellin'."

The snoring stopped. "What are you guys doing? Too much noise ..."

"Get up Stanley," Chandler said. "We need your help to open this door."

After more mumbling and the sound of sleeping bag zippers, the very uncombed Stanley appeared, clad head to toe in a furry orange onesie. "Yeah, It's Sydney's. Her stuff is warmer."

"Here, help us push." The three men put their weight into the effort. The old door creaked but did not move.

"Somebody's gonna have to go through the window," said Mike. He and Chandler looked at Stanley. "You're the smallest."

"He's skinnier," Stanley protested, pointing at Chandler.

Mike put his hands on his hips and looked down at him. "Yeah—but while you shovel out there, we'll be pushing from this side. I think you might fit right under my armpit."

"Besides, you can check on your car," added Chandler.

"OK—hang on, let me get some boots." Stanley returned to his corner. While he was rummaging, the women returned from the restroom. Elsa led the way. Rosie and AngelBaby followed, each supporting Etna by an arm on either side. She moved more slowly than ever, barely shuffling her feet. Sydney brought up the rear carrying a cosmetic case.

"Is she OK?" asked Chandler.

"We had a bit of a rough night," said Elsa. "I think playing the organ yesterday brought back some sad memories for Ettie."

Rosie looked at Chandler. "Her pulse is very slow. She needs medical attention immediately."

Sydney nodded, "She's right."

Chandler yelled, "Hey Stanley, hurry up—we need to get this door open."

"I'm coming, I'm coming." A few moments later Stanley emerged, clad in all the layers he could muster.

"Do you think he'll fit through the window?" Chandler asked Mike.

"Nope."

"OK man, you're gonna have to get rid of a couple of layers."

When Stanley began to protest, Sydney stepped in. "He's right, Stanley. And be quick."

Complaining, Stanley peeled out of his puffy yellow anorak and pea green pullover. "I'll freeze."

Sydney rolled her eyes. "We'll pass you your coat after you get out."

Pulling a chair to the window, Stanley climbed up to where he could almost get his shoulders through it. Chandler and Mike hoisted him through the rest of the way, then passed the shovel, coat and anorak through as well.

For a long time they heard nothing. The women flanked Elsa and Etna at the table, and Chandler passed around the now lukewarm chocolate. He thanked Rosie and AngelBaby for the Christmas treats and they smiled when he described adding a bit of candy to each cup. "Hot-chocolate-covered-mango-algae," said AngelBaby and started to giggle, but then looked again at the sisters and grew quiet.

Elsa sat quietly holding Etna's hand. Sydney and Rosie exchanged worried glances as Rosie checked the elderly woman's pulse again.

"Where is he? How long does it take to shovel snow?" Sydney said.

Mike returned to the front door and pressed his ear up against the scarred wood. "I think I can hear him now." Before long they could all hear cursing then scraping, then thumping. Mike beckoned Chandler to join him. "Let's try again."

The two men threw their shoulders into the door and it moved easily, knocking Stanley backwards. Cold air and his curses rushed into the room. The women huddled around Elsa and Etna, calling out, "Shut the door! Shut the door! It's too much cold!"

"First you want it open, then you want to shut it. Make up your mind ...!" Stanley stumbled back inside, covered in snow, rubbing his very red nose.

"Where's that shovel?" asked Mike. "We need to get Miss Etna some help right away."

"On the porch," Stanley replied. "Knock yourself out."

Mike rushed out the door and began digging a trail directly across the front of the porch and down the steps. Chandler grabbed the hammer and joined him on the porch, pulling boards off the front windows. The old dining room began to glow as light poured in through the grimy windows, illuminating every cobweb and tiny floating mote.

Etna squinted and opened her eyes. She slowly looked around the room. "Dust," she said and smiled. Then her head slumped to one side.

## Chapter 19

"Miss Etna! Miss Etna!" Rosie cried out. AngelBaby moved away from the table and held Elvis close.

Sydney looked at Rosie, "What should we do?"

Elsa took her sister's face in her hands. "Ettie, Ettie, can you hear me?"

"Lay her on the floor," Rosie said. "We have to be very careful, her bones can break so easily." AngelBaby ran for blankets. She stretched one out on the floor and rolled another to make a pillow for Elsa's head. "Don't put it there, we'll place it under her knees," Rosie said.

They laid her down and Rosie knelt beside her, placing her hands just below Etna's sternum as trained. Gently but firmly as she dared, she began chest compressions.

Elsa leaned over the table, head in her hands. "Dear God, not another one. I can't lose another sister. Not now, please God."

In the meantime, Mike continued to furiously shovel snow off the stairs. Pausing a moment to catch his breath, he called out, "Do you see a fallen tree anywhere?"

Chandler, prying off one last board, turned. All he could see in the parking lot were mounds of snow. "I guess it missed us. Thank God!"

"Yeah, Stanley would have let us know." Mike returned to his task.

As if on cue, the middle-aged man stuck his head out the door. "That old lady does not look good. Somebody's got to go for help."

Mike said, "What do you think I'm doing?" He reached the parking lot and began to consider which mound to attack first.

Stanley pointed. "Mine will go better in the snow," he said, "Start there." Chandler dropped his hammer and joined Stanley and Mike's efforts to dig out the Bentley. The sun shone intermittently as remnants of snowclouds blew by in the frigid wind. Even with three sets of hands it took nearly half an hour to free it enough to pry the front door open. Panting, the three men looked at each other. Who should go? Chandler shook his head no, and after a brief moment, Stanley handed Mike the keys. With a couple of quick instructions, Mike powered up the twin turbo engine. The windshield wipers swished away clouds of snow.

"Wanna come with me?" Mike asked Chandler. "Ride shotgun?"

The young man glanced back at Gran Gran's. "No. I think they're going to need me here. Be quick. Be safe."

Mike turned to Stanley, "You're the gambler. What are my odds?"

Stanley shrugged, "Can't say."

Mike mumbled, "Shut up, Stanley," under his breath and put the Bentley in Drive, then Reverse. He repeated the pattern rocking the heavy automobile back and forth until it broke completely free. A spray of snow shot out from the rear tires as he revved up the engine to plow through the deep powder that covered the parking lot. Stanley waved the shovel, ready to clear more of a path, but Mike shook his head. "I got it—this is a great car, man," and rolled up the window as he skidded away.

When Stanley and Chandler returned to the dining room, they found Sydney gingerly compressing Etna's chest while Rosie took a break. AngelBaby sat next to her aunt. "Will she be OK?" she kept asking.

"I don't know darling." Rosie looked grim. "We just have to keep going as long as we can."

Sydney came up for air. "Can you take a turn?" she asked Stanley.

He knelt down, but Rosie took his arm. "I am afraid a man will be too strong and break bones," she said. "We have to be so careful. I will go again now, Sydney—you rest, because I will need to trade back with you again soon." Red-faced, Sydney pulled away and Rosie stepped in to continue the compressions.

Etna's only motion was the jerking of her frail body under the pressure. Chandler took a seat beside her sister. He took her hand, and soon Elsa leaned on the young man's shoulder, weeping. "Its OK, Miss Elsa. We're doing all we can."

As the adrenalin from digging out his car wore off, Stanley began to feel colder than before. Sydney and Rosie were so engrossed in their life-saving rhythm, they seemed OK. But he noticed that AngelBaby, still holding Elvis, was shivering.

Stanley headed through the double doors into the kitchen and tried the stove. It would not come on. Anxiety building, he went out the back door and down the cellar steps. The stove was warm, but when he opened it up, dark. Their octopus had died.

## Chapter 20

Mike kept the Bentley in low gear as he made his best guess at where the road might lay. The landscape was filled in and smoothed over with a beautiful yet treacherous covering. It might be a foot deep in front of him then suddenly drop to six or ten, depending on how the wind had drifted the snow. He looked around to get his bearings, squinting in the glare of sunlight on snow. No cars, no trucks, no ambulances in sight. Gran Gran's was not far from the freeway—that was his best bet.

He turned the engine off for a moment to see if he could hear any kind of traffic anywhere. Everything was quiet. The world had stopped. "All I need is somewhere with a phone."

*All you need is a car like this,* said an old voice in his head. *Find the freeway and you're outta here. Set.*

Mike shook his head to clear the cobwebs. "No. Miss Etna needs help. These people trust me."

*Really?*

"Shut up." The burly man started the Bentley up again, appreciating the purr of its engine. Creeping along for almost a mile he saw a gas station sign sticking up out of a drift a few hundred yards away. "Easy, easy ..." He was gaining traction. "I need a snowplow on the front of this thing." He laughed thinking of the look on Stanley's face—then grew serious again.

"C'mon Mike. They're depending on you." He continued to inch forward. "Hurry up." He increased his speed, then slowly, slowly found himself plunging deep into a pile of snow that had filled up a hidden dip in the terrain. Mike threw the car into reverse. The big engine whined as wheels spun. It only dug him in deeper. He swore and pushed open the door. Snow tumbled in all over him and immediately formed small puddles as it melted across exquisite heated leather seats.

The big man half-swam half climbed up and out, following the car's path. He looked across at the gas station sign. *Shoulda brought those snowshoes.*

*****

At Gran Gran's, Rosie checked Etna's pulse again. The old woman had begun to rally a little, taking shallow breaths. "We must let her rest," Rosie said. Sydney was concerned about stopping the compressions, but Rosie insisted. "She is too frail. We need to give her body a chance."

Stanley moved to Chandler's side. "We've lost heat," he said in a low voice.

"What?" the young man looked up, alarmed.

"I went down to the cellar and checked," Stanley whispered. "The gas is off."

Chandler placed his hand on Elsa's shoulder and bent down to her ear. "Miss Elsa, I need to help Stanley with something. Can you stay here for just a bit? I'm sorry."

The woman nodded. He helped her lay her head down on the table.

Chandler followed Stanley into the kitchen. "You're right, it feels colder already," he said, rubbing his hands. I didn't notice it before."

"It's below freezing out there," Stanley replied. "We won't have water much longer either. The pipes will freeze up."

"I hope Mike can get some help."

"Yeah, yeah, Mike." The middle-aged man grunted. "We can't count on that. No telling how far he'll get."

"OK. Let me think. Water." Chandler turned on the kitchen faucet and stuck a pan under it. "Probably better collect as much as we can, while we can. And, would you go turn the faucets on in the restrooms? Just so they drip."

Stanley agreed and moved back through the double doors. Chandler pulled out every vessel he could find – jars, bowls, pots, and began filling them with icy tap water. A few minutes later Stanley returned with a large tin canister nearly half as tall as himself. Dented and dusty, it seemed intact. It even had a lid.

"Oh that looks good. What is it?"

"Old milk container. Farmers sold milk in 'em."

Chandler threw Stanley a rag. "See if you can get the dust out. I'm going to check on Miss Elsa."

He found the woman in the same position as before. He touched the side of her face, it was cool. She moaned a little but did not move her head. Sydney and Rosie were gently massaging Etna's arms and legs.

Chandler did not want to interrupt them. Instead he went to the pump organ area and retrieved a sleeping bag. Sydney looked up at the sound of him unzipping it, but nodded and went back to her work. He stretched it over Elsa, doing his best to tuck it around her. Chandler turned to the women and explained the heat situation. AngelBaby's eyes grew wide. Rosie murmured and crossed herself as Sydney said, "These ladies are the most vulnerable."

Chandler agreed. "I think we'll be OK. The storm is over. Rescue crews will start going out. But we have to do our best in the meantime. How's Miss Etna?"

"I don't know if we're making any difference," said Sydney.

"Rosie seems to know what she's doing," Chandler replied. "Do whatever she says. It may mean more than we know."

*****

Mike drew closer to the filling station. He was exhausted and could no longer feel his feet. Snow had drifted up against a retaining wall on one side leaving the entrance fairly accessible. No lights were on. It was what he had expected but still disappointing. He peered through the glass. It was not too dim to see an aisle of snacks to the left of the cash register. His stomach gurgled at the sight of food. He banged on the door. Nothing. He tried opening the door. Nothing. Cursing under his breath he turned toward the gas pumps and surveyed the parking lot. Then out of the corner of his eye he saw something familiar, but he would need to clear some snow to be sure ...

Yes. Beside the compressed air pump stood a weather-beaten payphone.

*Dinosaur* he thought. *Like me, probably doesn't work.* He lifted the receiver. Dial tone! He stuck his hands in his pockets. No quarters, dimes or nickels, not even a penny. "God, please. Please, please." Peering closer at the phone he saw a scratched yellow label. He could make out a "9." Then he figured out the rest of the message. "In case of emergency, dial 911." Holding his breath, he punched in the numbers. *Who in the world would even be around to answer?*

The icy handset felt cold up against his ear, but Mike pressed it close anyway. It was ringing.

*****

Gran Gran's atmosphere was noticeably cooler. Etna's pulse had dropped again and the women, shivering, resumed the compression cadence. Stanley had stacked up every flat surface in the kitchen with anything that would hold water. Chandler gave him a high five then said, "Time to start a fire." The two men returned to the dining room where Chandler had scooted a stack of the chairs close to the hearth.

"You sure about this?" asked Stanley.

"Absolutely."

Between the hatchet and hammer, they quickly reduced several chairs to kindling. Sydney placed the wood on the grate with care.

"Boy scout?" asked Chandler

"Yep."

"Wish we had Mike's lighter."

"I swiped some matches last night," said Stanley.

"Good."

Before long Stanley established a small blaze. The men then helped drag Etna on her blanket as close to the fire as they felt was safe. She was surprisingly heavy. Chandler tried to shake off the thought of *dead weight.* Elsa had fallen asleep and they hated to wake her. Sydney suggested setting up a table and chair so they could just half-walk, half-carry her to the warmer location and let her rest again. It worked. Elsa slumped back down across the tabletop and Rosie tucked the sleeping bag all around her.

Chandler said, "We've all got to stay as close to the fire as we can. We've collected up water in the kitchen in case the pipes freeze. If we're here for long, we may have to stop flushing toilets and save the water for drinking. I'm sorry about that."

"It was like that after Typhoon Yolanda," said Rosie. "Much hotter of course, but we had no electricity or running water for a very long time."

Chandler nodded. "We'll be fine. We just have to keep taking care of each other. Mike is out there getting help."

Chandler tended the fire as Stan gathered up the couple's belongings and set them closer to the hearth. Rosie and Angel-Baby did the same while Sydney tended to Miss Etna. When Chandler pushed through the double doors to retrieve Mike's borrowed blanket, he noticed his breath steaming. He began bringing water containers into the dining room as well. No need to lose heat.

Sydney beckoned to Rosie. "Come take her pulse again. I think I feel something." Rosie rushed to her side. Etna's face looked a little less ashen. She placed her fingers on the loose skin above the carotid artery, and felt a faint throb, then another. She crossed herself, then ever so gently pulled the elderly woman up into a seated position, as if cradling a child in her lap. "Please Miss Etna, stay strong." At her instruction, Sydney and AngelBaby each began gently massaging her legs and arms. "We must help her circulation."

# Chapter 21

"This is 911," said a tinny voice. "What's your emergency?"

"I'm just outside of Millersville, West Virginia," Mike yelled. His body had cooled way down after all the effort and he was shivering hard. "At a restaurant called Gran Gran's. Just off Highway 81. There's a group of us trapped—and two old ladies are really bad off." He could not feel his feet.

"I'm showing your location as a payphone at a gas station just off Highway 81, Exit 1 for Millersville. Can you please confirm?"

Mike coughed. "Yes, It's a Shell station. We have elderly ladies in our group and one of them just had a heart attack or something. She's not gonna make it if we don't get some help real soon. Do you guys have a helicopter or anything?"

There was a long pause at the other end of the line. "One moment, sir."

"I don't have a moment. I'm freezing. Old ladies are dying! Where are you? Who am I talking to?"

"Um, I'm in Cincinnati—but I'm connecting you to the local ..."

Mike swore. "I just crawled through a mile of snow on my hands and knees. The gas station I'm calling you from is closed and locked. I'm probably gonna freeze out here, my car is stuck in a snow drift, and you're in CINCINNATI?"

"Putting you on hold for one moment so I can connect you with the call center closest to you sir. Hang in there. Merry Christmas." With a click the tinny voice was replaced by a recording. But only for a moment. Then it went dead.

Mike swore again and threw the receiver down as hard as he could. It swung back and forth, loose and useless. No change to make another call, Mike pressed his fingers against his lips to keep his teeth from chattering.

The big man sank down in the snow. "This is such a crock. My whole life has been a mess and it's gonna end in a parking lot?" He thought of the sneer on his ex-wife's face every night when he got home from work. He thought of his football coach who shamed him in front of the team when he missed a critical play. He thought of his dad who promised again and again but could never seem to make it to a game. "Maybe I deserve to die in a parking lot. Who's gonna care?"

Then he thought of a group of people gathered around a fireplace and someone playing the guitar and singing. Another voice in his head said. *They care, and they need you.* Mike shook his head. It was as if someone had spoken to him, but he couldn't see anyone. He stood up and hung the receiver up back on the phone.

It immediately rang.

Trembling, Mike pulled it to his ear. "Hello?"

He was answered by an authoritative voice. "Are you at the Shell station just off Exit 1 on Highway 81 outside of Millersburg, West Virginia?"

Tears sprang into Mike's eyes, "Yes. Yes I am."

## *Chapter 22*

Life Flight Pilot Jordan Dylan glanced around the St. Agnes Hospital rescue crew room. Everyone was on high alert. Over the last two days, emergency response teams across three states had fought through white-out conditions and extreme cold. Pilots readied themselves to fly as soon as it was feasible. Finally, as of very early this Christmas morning, the storm had mostly blown itself out. Helicopters could begin attending to the growing backlog of emergency calls.

Most years, members of the rescue team on call would spend the day watching sports and movies. Maybe play a little poker. Eat some pizza. Earn time-and-a-half holiday pay for their twelve-hour shift. But the "storm of the century" was making this a very memorable Christmas. Extra crews and a heightened sense of risk reminded Jordan of flying Hueys in the gulf war. Adrenalin flowed and he loved it.

Jordan's turn came soon. He was responding to a 911 call made from a payphone in the northeastern corner of West Virginia. While the snowplow cleared a path outside, he ran the preflight checks on his EC-145 in a warm hangar. He had already thoroughly checked weather conditions. Coordinates were extrapolated from a Google map, but ultimately it would be up to him to locate the building where people were trapped. Snow complicated everything.

Jordan was well acquainted with the nurse and EMT who completed his crew, but no one made small talk today. It was the Life Flight pilot's job to get them on-site safely so they could address the patient situation, then get them back out safely to the best facility as fast as possible.

Visibility was decent, but Jordan would have to watch for ice, and of course trees and power lines. He had landed the EC-145 in plenty of tight spaces, but no one on the ground would mark out a landing zone for him. Not a great time to improvise. But that's why he flew. Not just anyone could, or would, do this job.

Once airborne, it didn't take the aircraft long to reach the edge of Millersville. Deep snow obliterated edges and contours that normally identified roads and buildings. Jordan ascended, literally for a bird's eye view. He scanned the area for a 70 by 150 foot building sitting on couple of acres just off Highway 81—with a parking lot. Without GPS, it would have been impossible.

The Life Flight pilot made a pass at three thousand feet. He could see the freeway, the Shell station, and what were probably a couple of fast-food places. Within a mile, he spotted a long building crouched against the hillside, surrounded by trees. Maybe?

On the second pass, he saw tiny figures jumping up and down and waving. "They better get out of the way," he mumbled as he began to descend.

*****

"That's a chopper!" yelled Sydney. "Mike must have gotten through to somebody!"

Chandler and Stanley rushed out to the porch just in time to see the blue and white Life Flight helicopter buzz over the top of Gran Gran's. They jumped up and down, waving and cheering. Sydney joined them.

"Watch out," she said. "He's gonna clear this parking lot so he can land. We'd better get back inside." She half-dragged, half-pulled the reluctant men through the door. They glued themselves to the windows to watch. "This is not an easy place to land," she said, "And no one's here to guide him. Dear God, please help."

Rosie, at Etna's side, crossed herself. AngelBaby did so as well. True to Sydney's word, they soon heard the roar of the pilot's return. Jordan hovered for a few moments directing hurricane-force winds, like an enormous snowblower, to clear a landing space.

Inside Gran Gran's it seemed as if the blizzard had returned. Thousands of cubic feet of snow in the parking lot blew out in all directions revealing bare gravel. Ice, dust and pebbles blew up along with it, scouring the parked vehicles. Jordan landed the chopper. It was now his job to wait and be ready to leave quickly. "Your Uber Air is here," he said.

Two figures bearing stretchers, heads bent low, ran toward the old restaurant.

*****

The nurse and EMT quickly examined Etna and Elsa, preparing them for flight. They maintained constant radio contact with their pilot so he could lift off as soon as possible with the new passengers.

"I tried to do my best," said Rosie, fighting the desire to hover.

The nurse, a stocky man in his thirties, paused as he adjusted Etna's oxygen bag. Her color was starting to return. "Nobody could have done anything better. This lady owes you her life."

AngelBaby hugged her aunt, who for the first time in a very long time openly wept. Sydney placed an awkward arm around her shoulder.

"We did good," she said. Rosie nodded, wiping the tears from her face.

We'll try to get you all out of here on the next round," said the EMT before helping the nurse transport Etna to the helicopter.

"That would be great," said Chandler. "There's one more guy too."

"The dog?"

"No. Our buddy Mike."

"OK."

When they returned for Elsa, she fought the stretcher, insisting she could walk to the helicopter. But the nurse and EMT prevailed. "You're going to have to ride in the stretcher anyway, might as well get in now." Chandler was impressed with their negotiating skills.

Jordan was eager to leave. It was going to be a busy day. But just as they were loading Elsa into the helicopter, a tow truck rumbled into the parking lot. It was pulling a Bentley. Mike hobbled out. Just behind the tow truck, an old Ford F-150 fitted with studded snow tires pulled up as well. A golden retriever leaped into the snow, followed by a vigorous white-headed man in his seventies.

Elsa called out, "Robert! Bertie!"

"Aunt Elsa! Are you OK? And what's this all about?" He waved a crumpled envelope at her.

Jordan yelled at his crew. "Time to go, guys."

"Tell you later dear, must catch a flight," Elsa called to him as the rescue team pulled her in and settled her with her sister.

# Chapter 23

After all the noise and flurry of Etna and Elsa's departure, the restaurant felt strangely quiet. Listening to the silence for a moment, Chandler realized why. The constant undertone of wind no longer moaned. He looked at the white-satin covered Christmas dinner table. It seemed strange to no longer have the elderly sisters in their midst. *I'll probably never see them again,* he thought, and felt sad for the loss.

His reverie was interrupted as Robert (or Bertie, as Elsa called him) joined the travelers around the hearth.

"So, Miss Elsa and Miss Etna are your aunts?" Chandler asked. He found himself using a formal, protective tone.

"Sure do. Thought they might be up here when I went by to check on them last night and found this." The man held up an envelope. Shaky letters on the front spelled out "Merry Christmas, Robert."

"They talked about you," Sydney offered up. She felt shy and quiet.

"I'm sure they did," the man smiled. He looked around the room. "Lots of memories here. So what happened?"

Stanley answered, "This team of ladies took care of your aunts for hours before the rescue 'copter got here."

"That guy was a heck of a pilot," said their new guest. "Aunt

Elsa looked OK, what about Aunt Ettie?  She was always the frail one."

Rosie spoke up. "It's hard to say, sir. We just did our best while we waited for help to come."

"Thank you," Robert said. "I am grateful to each one of you."

"There's one more," Chandler added. As if on cue, Mike limped slowly down the hall from the Men's room. Wrapped up in the pink and yellow polka dot blanket, he was still shaking water out of his bushy black hair and beard. Everyone started laughing, and clapping.

"What's going on?" said Mike, "Who's this guy? Are we still taking guests? Is that light still on?"

He pulled the last remaining chair up to the fire, while Chandler introduced the newcomer.

"That your dog?" Robert asked AngelBaby who was watching anxiously as Elvis and the retriever got acquainted.

"Yes, that's Elvis."

"They'll get along great. My dog's name is Silas."

"May I pet him?"

"Of course."

AngelBaby knelt in front of the big dog. "Hi, Silas," she said softly. Everybody laughed as he nuzzled her face, knocking her backwards.

"He knows a pretty girl when he sees one," laughed Robert.

Chandler could no longer control his curiosity. "So how did you know to look for your aunts here?"

"Made sense. This was their sister's place,"

"You mean their sister Erma?" said Sydney.

"Yes, Erma Elizabeth Evans was my mother. She moved up

here after their dad died. Needed to make a new start. She went from Erma to Betty. She was quite a lady, she was." The man bent down to pet Silas who had returned to his feet. "My mom was the new girl in town, and it did her a lot of good."

"Elizabeth Evans ... Betty Evans. Where have I heard that name?" asked Sydney.

Stanley yelled it out first, "Paw Paw Queen!"

Robert laughed. "Yes she was. The first year she moved up here the sheriff took quite a shine to her but never could get her to go on a date. Some say he rigged the contest. But, one way or another, my Mom was voted Paw Paw Queen, 1962." He looked around the room at the walls. "There used to be a photo around here somewhere. I was in that parade too, just behind her car, riding a pony, but that's not in the picture."

"So your mother was Gran Gran?" asked Rosie, rolling her R's beautifully.

"Yes. You might say that," said Robert. "She opened this place up on a shoestring and a prayer. In fact, Aunt Elsa and Aunt Etna brought the old organ over. There was a traveling preacher who occasionally came through on Saturday mornings and held services. Seventh Day Baptist I think."

Chandler nodded. "That's how they knew."

"Knew what?"

"Lots of things. Like, 'you'll find a bible in the organ seat,' and I did."

"Sounds like them," Robert chuckled. "A bunch of this old stuff came out of the farmhouse in Knoxville when they did a fancy remodel. My mom was glad to get it. Said it made things feel homey. Business finally took off for her when they expanded Highway 81."

He looked at Chandler. "But this place has been closed for years. What were you doing here?"

Chandler started to explain about the Angelino brothers and their investment plans, but Mike interrupted him.

"He turned the light on."

# *Epilogue*

Touseled, Early Morning Sherr handed Chandler a steaming cup of coffee. He followed her with his eyes as she took the seat across from him on her parent's front veranda, a deep cool red tile-floored refuge shaded by flowering vines. The air was a little muggy, but this early in the morning, it was cool and pleasant in the shade. A tall oscillating fan stood ready in the corner. It reminded Chandler of his grandmother Nonnie. No air conditioning at her house, ever.

It was hard to believe that just a few hours on a plane could transport a person from dreary winter to this bright corner of paradise. Chandler took a deep breath and smelled coffee and flowers and warm air.

"I have something I want to give you," Chandler said. "Sorry it's not wrapped or anything. So close your eyes and put out your hand."

Sherr laughed, "Last time a boy told me to do that, I got a frog."

"No frogs. I promise." She reached out her hand, palm up. "Other way." Sherr turned her hand over. He grasped a long slender finger and slipped a smooth cold ring part-way down. She opened her eyes wide. "You'll have to take it from there," he said.

"Oh my—where on earth did you get this?" Sherr drew her hand close to her face to examine the gift. "Is that an ..."

"Yes."

The deep green glow of an emerald set in white gold and tiny diamonds radiated against the bronze sheen of Sherr's deep tan.

"I'll have to do my nails if I wear that! Where ...? How ...?"

Chandler laughed. The ring fit her perfectly. "Those old ladies. Miss Elsa pulled me aside," he paused, choking back a little sob. "It was when I thought you had lost your mother. She reached into her pocket and pulled this out. She said, 'When you see your bride again, you give it to her. It belonged to my mother. Make it a memorial to hers.'"

"I don't know what to say."

"I didn't either. I thanked her, and when we figured out your mom was not dead, I tried to give it back, but she insisted. Then after, well, when her nephew Robert showed up, after everything happened, I tried to give it back to him too."

"He wouldn't take it?  This has got to be worth ..."

"Yeah, I know. No. He said he wanted us to have it, to honor the memory of his grandmother, his mother and his aunts."

Sherr reached up and hugged her husband. "I will always treasure this—and you," she whispered in his ear.

*****

That evening, following a huge meal of corn fritters, fresh fruit, *arroz con gandules*, roasted meats, rice pudding, *pasteles* and more, the extended Palacios clan gathered around the television to watch a New Year's Eve celebration "Live from

# Acknowledgements

It is great fun to bring characters and a story to life. Now for the cast of real-life characters who contribute more than they know to my happiness.

I am deeply indebted to my family members: parents and siblings—all writers (!) who have listened, read and sustained my efforts. My Rahab's Rope band-sisters laughed out loud when I read them the first few chapters at our annual retreat and kept asking for more—blessed fuel. Writerly friends, Eric Frugé, Pat Ham, and John Maust reviewed beta-versions and provided wise advice. Cindy Willey, brilliant, kind editor, cleaned up tortured punctuation *and* pointed out corn meal-related recipe nuances. She is heaven-sent! Cover designer, Rae House, somehow peeked in my brain and came up with the perfect image. Real-life rescue helicopter pilot Denver Gillham, son of Daniel, my amazing husband, shared real-life rescue helicopter details. Thank you for your service!

Deanie Cinnamon and Carol Lattuca, you have faithfully labored in prayer on my behalf. May Jesus, the original Christmas miracle, be honored by this attempt to shine light. Amen.

# About the Author

Jana Gillham spent her formative years in the Philippines, has been traveling ever since, and loves it. Her stories are inspired by musings on daily life.

She eventually settled in Lexington, Kentucky where she enjoyed two decades in corporate training and communications, then leapt off into the world of consulting and writing.

Jana is a co-founding member of the "eclectic" gospel band, Rahab's Rope. www.rahabsropeband.com.

In their "spare" time she and husband Dan, also a musician, are building Bright Berry Farm.

**Connect** with Jana at www.janagillham.com to inquire about speaking engagements, training needs and retreats.

To **receive the occasional short essay** in your inbox, follow her on Medium: Jana Gillham – Medium

* 9 7 8 1 7 3 3 0 0 0 5 1 2 *